"You've got me right where you want me, Princess. And you know I can't walk away."

"You mean, not without your story?"

Gabriel got up and came around the table, then lifted her out of her chair. "No, Princess, I can't leave because of you."

He saw a new kind of fear in her eyes. A fear of having loved and lost. "I don't know what you mean."

He tugged her close. "Yes, you do. You're a smart woman. Surely you can see it?"

She lowered her gaze. "See what?"

"This," he said, his fingers lifting her chin. "This, Lara."

Books by Lenora Worth

Love Inspired Suspense

A Face in the Shadows
Heart of the Night
Code of Honor
Risky Reunion
Assignment: Bodyguard
The Soldier's Mission
Body of Evidence
The Diamond Secret
Lone Star Protector
In Pursuit of a Princess

Love Inspired

†*The Carpenter's Wife*
†*Heart of Stone*
†*A Tender Touch*
Blessed Bouquets
   "The Dream Man"
*A Certain Hope
*A Perfect Love
*A Leap of Faith

Christmas Homecoming
Mountain Sanctuary
Lone Star Secret
Gift of Wonder
The Perfect Gift
Hometown Princess
Hometown Sweetheart
The Doctor's Family
Sweetheart Reunion
Sweetheart Bride

Steeple Hill

After the Storm
Echoes of Danger
Once Upon a Christmas
   "'Twas the Week Before Christmas"

†Sunset Island
*Texas Hearts

LENORA WORTH

has written more than forty books for three different publishers. Her career with Love Inspired Books spans close to fifteen years. In February 2011 her Love Inspired Suspense novel *Body of Evidence* made the *New York Times* bestseller list. Her very first Love Inspired title, *The Wedding Quilt,* won *Affaire de Coeur*'s Best Inspirational for 1997, and *Logan's Child* won an *RT Book Reviews* Best Love Inspired for 1998. With millions of books in print, Lenora continues to write for the Love Inspired and Love Inspired Suspense lines. Lenora also wrote a weekly opinion column for the local paper and worked freelance for years with a local magazine. She has now turned to full-time fiction writing and enjoying adventures with her retired husband, Don. Married for thirty-six years, they have two grown children. Lenora enjoys writing, reading and shopping…especially shoe shopping.

IN PURSUIT
OF A PRINCESS

LENORA WORTH

⬦ HARLEQUIN® LOVE INSPIRED® SUSPENSE

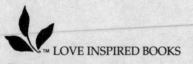 ™ LOVE INSPIRED BOOKS

ISBN-13: 978-0-373-67573-9

IN PURSUIT OF A PRINCESS

www.LoveInspiredBooks.com

Printed in U.S.A.

What is my trespass? What is my sin, that thou hast
so hotly pursued after me?
—*Genesis* 31:36

To Lavender and Landry—two special princesses!

ONE

"You'll probably get bored following me around, Mr. Murdock."

Gabriel managed a smile, his gaze traveling over the regal woman standing in front of him. "I can't imagine that, Princess Lara. Many men would give their eye teeth to have my job right now."

The princess stiffened at that comment. "I'm well aware of the paparazzi camped out down near the front gate, Mr. Murdock. Those photographers are more than willing to sell their souls—and mine— for a picture of me. Why, I'll never comprehend. I've accepted that, but I don't have to like it. However, having a photojournalist follow me around day by day is going to be a bit daunting. And as I said, you'll get bored. My life is not as exciting as the tabloids seem to think."

Gabriel didn't want to feel sorry for the beautiful woman standing by the fireplace, but the grief and doubt on her face did look real. And she had suffered a great loss. "I'm sorry," he said, wondering why he felt the need, "about your husband. In spite of my being a skeptic of the worst kind, I do believe you two were the real deal."

She turned and stood against the backdrop of the marble fireplace and an exquisite painting of an Arcadian village over the mantel, her expressive blue-green eyes holding him. "We loved each other. I don't care what the rest of the world thinks."

Or him. She didn't really care what he thought. And Gabriel didn't blame the woman. He'd read up on his subject enough to know the details. American heiress falls for European prince and the whole world goes wild with fascination at this match made in ratings heaven. In spite of the odds, they get married and will supposedly live happily ever after. But five years into their picture-perfect marriage, the prince is killed in a hunting accident. And the beautiful young princess is left grief-stricken and alone, to carry on their good works all over the world.

A widow for over two years now, Her Royal Highness Princess Lara Barrington Kincade had come home to New Orleans to continue her charitable work by holding an art fundraiser to benefit the Kincade Foundation and to continue building Kincade houses for the HRH Theodore Kincade Home Restoration Project in New Orleans.

Gabriel glanced up at the massive painting over the fireplace. He'd seen pictures of it in displays and magazines. A Benoit, painted in the late-nineteenth century by the French artist Jacques

Benoit. An authentic representation of the Arcadians who'd been forced out of Nova Scotia in 1755, but depicted in New Orleans in the true Arcadian art theme of a place of contentment and harmony. This, and the title *Arcadian Dreams,* made the painting bittersweet. A village within a dream— two distinct themes in one painting. And worth a lot of money, if his guess was right.

"The Benoit is stunning," he said to take her mind off the masses pushing at the gate. He noted a blinking light on the wall over the painting. A sensor for protection, no doubt.

"Yes." She turned to glance up at the painting. "It was a wedding gift from my husband."

So this was how her life played out. Priceless artwork and never-ending philanthropic events.

Gabriel had been assigned to follow the princess around and produce a photo spread with accompanying content. Right now she was preparing for a big art auction and reception to benefit Kincade House. He was supposed to be grateful that he'd been "given" this opportunity at the national magazine where he'd worked for ten years. "Given" being the loose term for punishment. According to his editor at *Real World News,* Gabriel had gone rogue one too many times to get the pictures and story he wanted.

Nothing like getting the job done while rubbing a third-world dictator and the Secretary of State the wrong way in order to get the best shots. But that wasn't why he'd been banished to New Orleans to do a fluff piece. He didn't want to think about the real reason he'd agreed to take this easy assignment.

Gabriel searched for the truth and he told it in his award-winning photographs and tell-it-like-it-is text. While the magazine owner and his editor had published his latest exposé with unabashed glee, they still had to make him pay to save face with the government.

And this was their way of doing that. This was torture for a true reporter and photojournalist. But what a beautiful torture.

Remembering another woman in another place, he put on a blank expression and tried not to chafe at being in such a straightlaced setting.

"Call me Gabriel," he said, thinking even though this was child's play, at least the subject matter was…lovely to look at. The princess was honey-blonde and photogenic, no doubt about that. But Gabriel wanted to get down to the real woman behind that chignon and those designer pumps.

"Gabriel," she said, coming to sit down on the settee across from the overstuffed chair where he'd landed. "So I understand you have a home here in New Orleans, too."

"Yes." He nodded, stared at the hot tea growing cold in front of him. "I grew up here, and when my mother died, I inherited a town house in the Quarter. So it's not far from your home. One of the many reasons this assignment enticed me."

That much was true at least. He didn't mind some downtime in New Orleans. Good food, good jazz and a mirror of his own conflicted soul. Now he had a beautiful woman to admire, too.

"I'm sorry about your mother. Were you close?"

He wanted to say no, not really. His artistic, temperamental mother had stayed single and had never told him who his father was. Maybe that was why he'd become so nomadic. Seemed he was always searching for the truth. Instead he said, "We grew to be close as we both matured."

She smiled at that. "Sometimes, growing up is hard work."

"Yes." He didn't want to discuss his relationship with his mother. "Anyway, I have the town house here. So I'll have my darkroom and some other equipment stashed away."

"That's convenient," she said, sipping her tea with her pinkie precisely in the right place. "My parents bought this house when I was a toddler. They split their time between New Orleans and several foreign locations since my father was a diplomat—great for them and educational for me. After they retired and moved to Virginia, they left this house to Theo and me. We spent part of our honeymoon here." Her vivid eyes went blank for a second. "I rarely get back here but this fundraiser is important. I want to continue the work Theo and I started in New Orleans."

Gabriel finally lifted the tea and took a swallow.

Bitter and tangy, the tepid liquid coated his dry throat. "New Orleans will certainly benefit from your efforts. This city needs all the help it can get after that flurry of hurricanes a few years back."

She inclined her head, her pearl teardrop earrings trembling against her skin. "We started this foundation a year after the last big hurricane."

Gabriel glanced around the big square parlor. "Did your home suffer any damage?"

"A good bit, but we moved most of the artwork before the storm and when we returned we rebuilt the house. I have a friend who rents the carriage house, but she's on her honeymoon right now. Esther married a renowned adventurer and archaeologist—Cullen Murphy. You might have heard of him?"

Gabriel grinned. "Heard of him and had the pleasure of meeting him and the lovely Esther when we did a magazine shoot on the Levi-Lafitte Chocolate Diamond. They mentioned several locations in New Orleans, but obviously left your estate out for the sake of privacy. Amazing find, that."

"Yes, Esther told me all about their big adventure. Lots of danger and intrigue, but they found the diamond and now it's in a museum in Washington, I believe."

"That's right. So you know Esther and Cullen. It's a small world."

"Too small at times," she said.

When a nearby cell phone rang, she excused

herself and hurried to pick it up, surprising Gabriel. He figured she had servants in every corner to take care of such tasks. He'd already met one of them, a strange little lady who had introduced herself as Deidre. Deidre had brought him into this room and…disappeared immediately. He'd seen others, bodyguards and drivers and security teams. He'd been fully vetted before he could even take on this assignment and then a nice burly escort had met him, frisked him and brought him here. Gabriel had no doubt he was being watched even now.

"Hello?" Princess Lara turned toward him with an apologetic smile. "Hello?" Frowning, she hung up. "Wrong number."

Gabriel wondered about that and why Deidre wasn't fielding the phone calls. "Could be. Or maybe the photographers lined up outside are taking turns to see if you're still in the house."

"I told Deidre I was expecting some very important calls, but if this keeps up I'll have to let her run interference."

Ah, that explained that, then. A self-sufficient princess. He liked her already. But she could be a bit naive, too. "You know the paparazzi have a way of getting even the most private of numbers."

She came to sit back down, a pretty frown marring her face. "You know all the tricks, I see."

"A few." He finished off the tea, then stared over at her. "But I want you to understand, while I'm trailing around after you, I will respect your privacy and your work. You'll have full approval on any and all photographs that make the cut for *RWN* magazine as well as the accompanying content, I can assure you."

She did the chin-lifting thing again—her way of nodding, he decided. "And when will we officially begin?"

Gabriel looked at his watch. "I'm on the clock right now."

She stood as if to dismiss him but stopped. "Would you like to stay for dinner? We can go over my schedule. It can be a bit daunting if you're not used to it."

Surprised, Gabriel shrugged. He had to eat. Might as well get to know her over good food. "If it's not too much trouble, I'd appreciate that. I like to be prepared so, yes, a schedule would be great."

"I'll go and tell my assistant to ready our meal, then."

Gabriel wondered if he wanted to eat anything cooked by Deidre. The little woman was so somber and skittish, she gave him the creeps. And it took a lot to scare Gabriel Murdock.

Maybe he should be more wary of the princess he was about to get to know on a personal level. After all, beauty and grace could hide a multitude of sins.

The man was sinfully handsome.

Lara took another bite of the catfish smothered in crawfish étouffée, her stomach almost recoiling at the rich New Orleans food. Her nerves weren't the best these days. Since Theo's death, she'd been an emotional wreck and her doctors had given her more sedatives and antidepressant pills than she cared to remember. But the pills didn't help the never-ending ache in her heart. She pretended to take them, but most of the prescribed medication went down the drain. She had to have a clear head for the task ahead.

Tonight, she thought this distress might have more to do with the man sitting beside her at the antique Queen Anne table than the spicy food or a lack of pills. But those annoying hang-up calls hadn't helped her nerves, either.

Gabriel Murdock ate the food with gusto, his manners impeccable even while he enjoyed each bite. He was buff and in shape, so he could afford the spicy sauce and crusty catfish. His hair was dark and curly, with just a hint of gray near the temples. His eyes were an interesting shade of brown—almost golden at times. She'd heard many tales regarding the renowned photojournalist, some of them good and some of them bad. "Infamous" was how Deidre had described him. He traveled light and often, never stayed in one place for long and was rumored to be one of the best at getting a story with just one shot of his camera. But he had also been involved in exposing corruption and righting wrongs by being nosy. Malcolm had thoroughly researched the man, but had given his okay to this assignment.

"He'll be aware and on high alert," Malcolm had told her. Apparently these were impressive qualities in a good photojournalist. "He tends to dig deep to get his stories."

Deidre, on the other hand, warned Lara almost immediately.

"You'd best watch out for that one, ma'am," her overprotective assistant had cautioned. "Especially since you refused to bring a full detail with us."

"I'll be perfectly fine," Lara had replied. "I don't want guards hovering around me day and night. Our smaller team is sufficient. I need some freedom for a change."

"Yes, ma'am."

But Lara knew that the guards were out there somewhere, watching in spite of her need to break free. She wasn't so complacent as to think they had let her get away with her request so easily. She would always be a member of the royal family, even if her husband was no longer alive. She owned a mansion full of priceless artifacts and antiques, too. And that meant protection, since even now she had death threats and stalkers and all sorts of other worries to consider. Now was not the best time to have a photographer trailing her, but it couldn't be helped. She needed publicity for her cause. She'd have to be very careful about what she revealed to him, however.

But this one—Gabriel—seemed capable of handling anything they might encounter together. The man had been embedded with American troops in the Middle East, had trailed drug lords and terrorists undercover through the jungle to get the real story. He seemed to be content and confident in his own skin, even if his eyes did hold a rim of sadness. Lara felt a strange sense of peace, the first real peace she'd felt since Theo's death.

"This is really good," Gabriel said now. "My compliments to the chef."

"We have a good friend who is an accomplished chef," Lara replied, happy that he approved of the cuisine. "Even though Deidre is an excellent cook, Herbert insists on cooking for me when I'm in town. He so enjoyed teaching Theo all about Creole and Cajun cooking and the difference between the two."

"Spoken like a true Louisiana soul," Gabriel replied. "Did your husband enjoy eating the local dishes?"

"Oh, yes. He was willing to try anything. Even alligator meat and frog legs—I've never managed to acquire a taste for either."

The room went quiet as she remembered the good times she'd had with Theo. Finally, she glanced over at Gabriel and realized he'd put down his fork. "I'm so sorry. It's just...I miss him."

"I understand." He pushed his plate away. "From everything I've seen and heard, he was a good man."

"The best." She blinked away her grief with a quick flutter of her lashes and a flash of regret in her expression. "Now, let's move on, shall we? We have a lot to discuss. I'll show you some of the other art pieces—some I own and others on loan for the reception we'll hold here before the official show in the Quarter. As you know, I intend to be in New Orleans for at least three months. How long do you plan to...shadow me?"

He gave her a direct look. "I have the whole month."

One month, weeks and weeks, with this nice-looking man. Lara had to wonder if they'd get along, or if they'd wind up getting on each other's nerves.

"Don't look so glum," he said, as if reading her mind. "I don't bite. I know my job and I know my place."

She shook her head. "But I want you to feel comfortable. I want you to get the story right. You know, a lot of people think I'm just interfering, trying to get publicity or pity, anything you can think of. They can't seem to grasp that I lived here for many years and I want to give back to the place I love."

"I don't care what other people think," he replied.

"I'm here to follow you and to capture that essence that makes the world so fascinated with you."

"I'm not so sure I have an essence," she retorted, embarrassed by the way he looked at her. "I do care or I wouldn't be here."

"I believe you."

"Then let's get started. I'll have Deidre bring dessert and we'll eat while we compare."

For the next couple of hours they nibbled on their mini-fruit tarts and drank more coffee while they went over the details of the next week.

Finally, Lara glanced up and noticed the time. "It's close to eleven. You must be exhausted."

"No, I'm good."

He gave her that look again, the one that made her blush. Was he one of those night owls who needed little sleep?

"But I imagine you're tired."

"I am rather fatigued," she said, patting at her hair. She longed for a bubble bath and a good night's sleep.

They both stood up and Lara was about to escort him to the door when Deidre walked in with a package. "Ma'am, I found this at the back door."

"The back door? That's odd. No one alerted us." Lara took the square box and began to open it, thinking it might be the stationery she'd ordered from her favorite local paperie. "Do you mind if I check on this?" she asked Gabriel. "This might be the addressed invitations for the gala and silent auction we're having at an old mansion in the Quarter. We had a typo in the first batch, so they were going to do a rush order to get them here in time."

"Of course not." He sat back and studied his notes.

Deidre watched as Lara tugged at the box. "I'll put it away after you're finished, ma'am."

Lara pulled back the tissue paper and gasped, then backed against a chair, the box still in her hands.

Gabriel jumped up and grabbed the box. "That's not invitations."

Deidre peered over into the open package. "Oh, my. Oh, ma'am, I'm so sorry. I'll take it away immediately."

Lara nodded, put her hand to her throat. "Yes, please do."

"No, don't touch it." Gabriel pushed Deidre away. "We need to alert security."

"No. I don't think—"

"Yes," Gabriel said. "Just as a precaution."

After Deidre turned away to pull out her phone, Lara regained some of her composure and stared up at Gabriel. "I think someone is trying to warn me away from New Orleans."

He frowned, his gaze centered on her. "I think you might be right."

She closed her eyes and thought about what she'd seen in that box. It was just superstition, nothing else. Or had the horror she'd feared started already? Had her tormentor already arrived in New Orleans?

Gabriel seemed to be as concerned as she was. He took her hand away, forcing her to open her eyes. "Who do you know that would send you a voodoo doll with a pin through the heart, Princess?"

TWO

"Really, this isn't necessary."

Gabriel glanced over at Lara Kincade, surprised that she had not wanted to call her security team or the police. He and Deidre had finally convinced her to call her head of security.

"But it is. You have to take these things seriously even if you think they're pranks." He studied the little satin-covered doll with the big blue eyes and the blond yarn hair. "A voodoo doll is a signal, prank or no prank."

"I get this sort of 'signal' all the time," she said, one arm wrapped around her waist, propping up the other arm she had lifted to her face. She stood just that way, her fingers curled against her chin, while she studied the red-satin-lined box with the odd-looking little figurine lying inside. "When I was young, I saw one of these in a store window down in the Quarter. I begged for it, but my mother refused to let me have it. She told me it wasn't the kind of doll with which a little girl should play."

"It's not the kind of doll a grown woman should fool around with, either," Gabriel replied, his English not nearly as proper as hers. But then, he'd practically grown up down in the Quarter. He'd learned street smarts long before he'd studied photography, and he'd learned how to read people long before he'd studied journalism. And something about the woman standing in front of him didn't wash. She was too calm, too practiced. "You can't take any chances."

"They're on the way," Deidre said as she bustled around the room with a cell phone in her hand, her dark eyes wide with concern. "Ma'am, I'm so sorry."

"Deidre, you did nothing wrong," Lara replied, her eyes still on the package. "Stop apologizing and please stop pacing."

Deidre skidded on the spot but looked anxious all the same. "I should have waited until we'd had the package checked by one of the guards. I know the protocol."

"Deidre, remind me again—you didn't see who delivered this?" Gabriel said.

Deidre looked at him, then glanced toward the princess.

"Go ahead, answer him," Lara said on a gentle voice. "He's here to observe and take pictures, but he might be able to help."

"I didn't see anyone, and Herbert has already gone home so we can't ask him."

"Maybe we can call him. He might have taken the package." Gabriel wanted to reassure the girl. "I'm trying to piece things together before we call the police."

"The police?" Lara glared at him and shook her head. "I told you, no police. My head of security—"

A door down the hallway burst open and a tall bull of a man with tight graying curls muscled his way into the room. "Your Highness, we've alerted the team. We've got guards stationed all around the property."

"—is here right now." Lara moved away from the offending package but waved her hand toward it. "Thank you, Malcolm. There it is. This is what all the fuss is about. Quite silly, honestly."

Malcolm glanced at the voodoo doll, then turned to stare at Gabriel. "What's your take?"

Gabriel lifted his eyebrows, surprised that anyone cared about his thoughts on this. He didn't want to be involved in whatever was going on. He'd already met Malcolm Plankston through a thorough vetting interview that had left him wondering if the man would even let him go on with his assignment. Apparently, he'd been approved. "I take it very seriously," he said. "I've encouraged Princess Lara to call the police."

"And I've discouraged that notion," Lara retorted. "It's another of those odd pranks people tend to play on me. Some of the locals don't appreciate my interest in rebuilding New Orleans. They tend to forget that I lived here for many years myself."

"I agree with Mr. Murdock," Malcolm said. "The authorities need to hear about this. You've stirred up publicity with this art fundraiser and the public knows you're here. You're vulnerable."

"No," Lara said, shaking her head. "The local police will laugh in my face and tell me this is just someone's way of welcoming me home. You know how they scorn my presence here. They think I'm just another celebrity wanting media attention. I won't bring them in on this and that's final."

Gabriel knew not to argue with a woman who stood tapping her expensive-looking leather pump against the polished wood floor. And he knew not to overstep his position by urging her head of security to go against her wishes.

Malcolm lifted the doll with a pair of tweezers that somehow appeared out of nowhere. Probably from inside Deidre's deep pockets. The woman kept pulling things out of each one like a magician pulling rabbits out of a hat.

"Odd little thing," Malcolm said, his mustache twitching while he seemed to stop blinking. "I'll take it out to the shop and analyze it, but I think it's harmless." He dropped the doll, then turned to the princess. "I won't call in the New Orleans police this time, Your Highness. But if anything else out of the ordinary occurs, I will have to do my duty and report it."

"Agreed," Lara replied, clearly relieved that she wouldn't have to deal with anyone else official tonight. "I promise I'll keep you apprised. Deidre and I will be diligent on that account, I can assure you."

Malcolm cast a furrowed glance toward Deidre. "I assume you will make sure this never happens again."

Deidre's eyes misted. "You have my word on that, sir."

"Good," Malcolm the Intimidator said in his firm, gruff, no-nonsense voice. "Your position here could very well depend on it."

Lara walked around the desk and took Deidre's hand. "It's all right. You are not going to be dismissed. Go on to bed and get some rest. I'll be fine."

Deidre rushed out of the room, her brown ponytail bouncing, her walnut-colored loafers squeaking.

Lara had a serene look on her face when she reached out her left hand and placed it on Malcolm's gray wool suit. "Don't ever reprimand Deidre in that way again, Mr. Plankston. Do I make myself clear?"

Malcolm swallowed, gulped and nodded. "I meant no disrespect, ma'am."

"Good night, Malcolm."

And the man was officially dismissed.

Which left Gabriel alone with a princess. An ice princess.

"Impressive," he said, rocking back and forth on his boots. "I'll have to remember not to get on your bad side."

She gave him an emerald-tinged stare. "Deidre has been with me since the day I married Theo. She's a dear girl—not much younger than me, really—a bit shy but very efficient. I won't have Malcolm bullying her since his team seemed to have entirely missed this delivery's arrival. He knows this wasn't her fault. I'm the one who insisted on relaxing my security while I'm here. I'm the one who wanted a little more privacy and a lot less formality."

Gabriel could understand her need for privacy, and he was pretty sure she should learn to relax a little more. But she was a princess, after all. "You're known the world over. Privacy is a hard commodity to come by, especially when someone as famous and well loved as you comes to New Orleans. That's the proverbial fishbowl way of living, Your Highness."

"That is a way of living that I have found very wearisome, Mr. Murdock. And please, call me Lara."

"As long as you call me Gabriel," he reminded her with a soft twist of a smile. "And it's time for me to go, too. Are you sure—"

"I'm fine. If I know Malcolm, he'll have a guard at the front door to make sure you get out safely and I stay in safely. I'll show you out."

She walked him to the door, her heels clicking in a dainty princess way. "I suppose I'll see you tomorrow."

"That's the plan." He turned and took her hand. "Thank you for tea and dinner and…a bit of excitement."

"Don't get used to that," she said on a soft smile. "My life is not as exciting as the world might think."

Gabriel bid her good-night, thinking she was wrong on that.

And as he tipped his hand to the burly guard hovering on the front veranda, he was pretty sure the excitement was just beginning.

Lara sat at her dressing table in her upstairs bedroom, staring at her reflection in the mirror. With no makeup and her hair down around her shoulders, she looked drawn and fatigued. Not exactly the image the world wanted to see.

She didn't care about that right now. She only saw the shadow of a mourning widow in her gilded mirror. And so much more. How did she explain to the world that she was tired of being a princess and that she only wanted to be herself, free and unencumbered by rules and protocol and regulations and proper procedures?

Lara turned from her brocade-covered stool and tugged her cashmere robe around her. It was early spring in the South, but the nights could still be cool. She paced over the hundred-year-old, hand-woven rug centered in the sitting area of the big, comfortable bedroom then went to the French doors and stared out into the back garden. Her mind fluttered here and there like a butterfly.

Esther and Cullen had gotten married right here in the garden. She'd insisted on giving them a reception to remember, and they'd pulled it off without too many problems with the media. Friends of a princess getting married didn't carry nearly as much weight as a princess getting married. Or remarried. The tabloids had a new story every week on that one. By the latest count, she should have been remarried about four times at least.

But she had yet even to go out with a man, let alone consider marrying one.

She thought of Gabriel Murdock and felt a strange tapping in her heart. He was certainly handsome in a swarthy, swaggering way. The man looked like a map of life, world-weary and scarred, well traveled and frayed, and interesting.

Too interesting. When he'd taken her hand, a pleasant warmth had moved through her and reminded her she was still a woman.

Her cell hummed. She didn't recognize the number. "Hello?"

"I got your invitation."

"And I got your gift. You can't scare me."

"I'm not trying to scare you. I'm trying to help you."

"By threatening me?"

"I don't know what you mean."

Lara put her hand to her heart. "Good, because you have the answers I need, so I won't fall for any tricks. I'll see you at the gala." She let out a breath. "And please quit making hang-up calls. It's juvenile."

"Is that all you have to say after all this time, Lara?"

"Yes. Good night."

Lara moved around the room, turning off lamps, her hands trembling. She kept going back over the day's activities, wondering how that package had gotten past security. And wondering how *he* had found her private cell number.

Putting her unwanted guest out of her mind for now, Lara regrouped and looked at her day-planner. Today had been busy, but tomorrow would be jam-packed. And she'd have Gabriel Murdock trailing her with every task. Was she really ready for that kind of up-close scrutiny? And by a man who seemed to read her like a book and look through her carefully controlled facade to see her deepest, darkest fears and secrets?

She thought about the man who'd just called her. It had been a long time since she'd seen him or heard from him. And she'd been biding her time until she could see him once again. "I can do this," she whispered. "I have to do this."

A shudder tiptoed down her spine.

"Remain calm and carry on," she repeated. That

used to be a joke between Theo and her. It was the mantra of a great queen and it did apply to the average commoner, too.

"That's me," Lara whispered as she climbed in bed and tugged at the last light. The room went dark on her fears and worries. She'd been a commoner, but a wealthy, well-heeled one at that. Money and prestige could open a lot of doors. Having a social pedigree that went back to the founding fathers didn't hurt, either. But even so, when the announcement of her marriage had been made, she'd been analyzed, studied, prodded and trained in everything from etiquette to speaking in public to greeting people to writing a proper thank-you card, all of which her mother had already trained her on anyway.

Being a princess was much harder than being a woman.

Right now, however, she mentally pushed her princess away and, being a woman, thought about the fascinating man with whom she'd shared her dinner. And wondered why she'd invited him to stay for a meal. That hadn't been on the agenda.

But then, neither had receiving that hideous gift. The voodoo doll only brought back bad memories of other times when she'd been afraid and full of doubts. Maybe this had nothing to do with that. Or it could have everything to do with that and the phone call she'd just received. She missed Theo, but she was determined to live life on her own terms.

And she was determined to find answers to the questions that had haunted her since Theo's death.

Obviously, after receiving that cryptic call, she understood the little voodoo doll had something to do with her nosing around where she shouldn't.

Lara punched her pillow, hating this time of the day when she felt so alone, so lonely, so unsure of anything but how much she missed her husband. Telling herself to get a grip, she pushed out of her mind that image of the little grinning doll with the pin stabbed through her heart.

"You can't pierce my heart," she whispered to the night. "My heart has already been broken."

But she intended to find the man who'd killed Theo. And she intended to do that here in New Orleans, with the world watching.

She drifted off to sleep thinking of her husband and Gabriel Murdock. Trying to hold one close in her memories and trying to push the other one back into a proper place, she finally went from being awake to being in a dream that ran through her head like a vivid movie, complete with voodoo and warnings from Deidre and Malcolm and with a man standing in the shadows, holding a camera.

The man called to her and Lara tried to reach him. He threw down the camera and reached out a hand. But she couldn't quite grasp his fingers.

She woke up near dawn thinking of her husband.

But the man in the dream had been Gabriel Murdock.

Lara lay there pushing at the covers, her body still exhausted from running through that mist, her memories as wild and colorful as the images in her mind.

A piercing scream sounded through the night, bringing her up and out of her bed. Grabbing her robe, Lara rushed to her door and followed the hallway to the sound of the scream.

Deidre's room.

But before Lara could open the door, Malcolm and two bodyguards were there with guns drawn.

"Step back, Your Highness," Malcolm said, his beefy arm blocking her way. "It might not be safe."

He knocked and called out. "Deidre?"

No answer.

"Go and check on her," Lara demanded, impatient with the head of security.

Malcolm motioned to the two guards. They were about to break the door down when Deidre opened it and ran straight into Lara's arms.

"What happened?" Lara asked, holding the younger woman.

Deidre lifted up, her dark eyes wide, her hair unbound and curly around her face. "I heard a noise on the upstairs balcony, ma'am. Someone walking, I'm sure. Then I saw a shadow near my window."

Lara held tight to the frightened girl. "Are you sure?"

Deidre bobbed her head, her words shaky. "Very sure. A man was standing there."

Malcolm put his big arms across his chest. "So you screamed?"

"Yes."

"But you didn't answer when we came to the door."

"I was still frightened."

He motioned again to the two men. "Search the balcony and the grounds."

Lara took Deidre by the arm, her own jitters making her shaky. "Come with me. We'll sit awhile and I'll make us some chamomile tea."

Deidre looked mortified. "Ma'am, you don't need to wait on me. I'm…okay."

"You are not okay," Lara countered. "Malcolm, we're going down to the kitchen. Could you make sure a guard is nearby while we brew our tea?"

"Certainly, Your Highness. But please let us secure the house before you wander around."

Lara nodded. "Deidre, let's get you a robe from your room."

The girl followed Lara into the room and stood by the door, staring out into the night. "I saw a man there, Miss Lara. I promise."

"I believe you," Lara replied. She helped Deidre with her robe. "Did the man try to get into your room?"

"No. He just stood there. When I screamed, he ran away."

Lara took in the information but said nothing.

She wouldn't allow Deidre to see her fears. That might put the girl over the edge.

But when they were turning to leave the room, something caught Lara's eye. "Just a moment, Deidre. Stay there by the door, please."

Deidre nodded. Lara walked to the open door that led out onto the balcony, careful to stay on the edge of the sheer lace curtains. Peeking around the lace, she saw something through the moonlight, lying there on the planked floor. The guards had rushed right past it. Another package, this one bigger than the first one.

Another delivery. But how in the world had the intruder planned to get that box inside? And what if he'd been looking for her room instead of Deidre's?

THREE

Gabriel knew something was wrong the minute he rounded the corner the next morning. He'd taken the streetcar to *RWN* magazine and then walked the rest of the way to the Kincade estate since it was such a gorgeous spring day.

But that notion ended when he saw two NOPD cruisers parked inside the gated driveway and a whole passel of reporters and onlookers stationed outside the closed gate. Pulling out the smaller of his two cameras and his phone, he dialed Deidre's cell so she could open the gate for him. He held the phone to one ear, clicked away and got some one-handed shots of the cruisers and the growing crowd at the gate.

But Deidre didn't answer. A male voice greeted him. "Hello?"

"Uh, I was looking for Deidre Wilder. I'm Gabriel Murdock. I have an appointment with Princess Lara this morning."

"Hold on." He heard shuffling and voices. "You're clear. Someone will come and escort you inside."

"Uh, thanks."

Gabriel shifted his equipment pack and bypassed the other photographers gathered beyond the gate, then waited where he could see the entryway. When a uniformed officer came out and punched in the code for the walk-through gate next to the driveway, there was a rush of people behind Gabriel.

The officer held up his hand. "Sorry, no one else allowed. This man has special clearance."

Moans and groans and foul language ensued behind Gabriel, followed by desperate questions: "Was anything stolen last night? Is the princess safe in New Orleans? Why are you here? Was anyone arrested? Will the princess make a statement to the press?"

Gathering that there had been a break-in attempt last night, Gabriel hurried through the gate and didn't look back at the agitated crowd. He'd been in worse jams. And he did have an official pass, which he flashed at the officer just for good measure.

But getting special treatment had stirred up the paparazzi. He'd probably hear about this in the news later.

"What happened?" he asked the stoic officer, hoping to verify what he'd heard from the reporters at the gate.

"An intruder last night."

And that would be all he'd get from that one. "Thanks."

He made his way behind the policeman into the side entrance, where a small porch was tucked behind a heavy canopy of banana fronds. This entryway led to the mudroom and kitchen.

And that was where he found Lara sitting with Deidre.

"Good morning," he said, glancing around at the guards and police officers. "Brunch?"

Lara got up, her expression as serene as ever, her hair back in its chignon, her light blue linen pantsuit not daring to wrinkle. "We had a scare last night. Deidre saw someone on one of the upstairs balconies, out by her window." She glanced around, then lowered her voice. "He left another package."

Not good news. "What was in the package?"

She shrugged, gathered her arms against her stomach. "It's another oddity." Motioning toward the breakfast table, she walked him over. "Sit down and I'll get you some coffee and explain."

Deidre, looking drawn and unkempt, jumped up. "Let me do that, ma'am."

Lara nodded, then sank into a cushioned chair. Gabriel sat down across from her. In the bright sunlight coming through the wall-to-wall bay windows that gave a full view of the back garden, she looked tired and...lost. Still lovely, but at least now he knew she was fairly normal. Wasn't everyone tired and lost anyway?

"The box, Lara?"

She sent a quick glance toward the swarm of men roaming up and down the stairs. "We can't go up to see it. They're taking photos and logging it as evidence. And they don't want us to disturb the scene—which really is only the balcony and the package."

"So the package is still where someone found it?"

"I saw it after I heard Deidre screaming. It was left on the balcony outside her room."

She waited until Deidre brought him coffee and a plate with muffins and cheese. The fidgety girl took her own dishes to the sink and busied herself with cleaning the kitchen. Lara continued, "It's a replica of one of the art pieces I showed you last night. The Benoit." She stopped, shook her head.

"But?"

She blinked, looked away to the right. "But it's not really the same portrait. I know it looks familiar but I can't place it. It's as if someone is trying to copy the Benoit's style."

Gabriel's instincts kicked in and he got that coiling knot inside his stomach, the knot he always got when he was onto something no one had been expecting. "Did anyone else see this intruder?"

"No. Deidre saw a shadow. The person ran when she screamed."

"Do you know if Deidre talked to Herbert about the first package?"

Looking surprised, she shook her head. "Deidre

mentioned that this morning, but no. He didn't answer her calls or messages."

Deidre had brought her the first package last night. No one else had seen that one delivered. And Deidre hadn't been able to get in touch with the chef last night to see what he might know.

Now Deidre had seen an intruder who'd conveniently left yet another package near her room? Coincidence or carefully planned attack?

Gabriel didn't believe in coincidences.

No wonder the girl scurried and jumped like a squirrel. She was obviously in on this gig. But why?

"So this replica—what is it? What's it about?"

Lara leaned forward. "It's another Arcadian dream. A group of Arcadians gathered by a large boat. The boat is sailing away through clouds and cherubs. Shepherds are watching from the sky. It's a sad portrait of the hardship the Arcadians had to endure, wrapped inside a beautiful dream."

He nodded. "Yes. So someone obviously knows you own a Benoit. And that it's worth close to a million dollars."

She lifted her chin in acknowledgment. "Yes. This one reminds me of that. Same technique, same dreamlike Arcadia backdrop with the Louisiana Arcadians featured. A pretty good representation but—"

"But what?" Gabriel felt the hairs on the back of his neck rising. A sure sign that this was bigger than just following around a princess. Suddenly, he had a real story going. But this wasn't supposed to be complicated. He wasn't ready for complicated again. Not yet.

"Oh, my." She got up, paced the floor, cast several covert glances over her shoulder.

He followed her. "Lara, tell me so I can help."

"Back in the early sixties, it was discovered that there was a set of three Benoit paintings in a quaint little museum in the Quarter. No one knew the value, not even the museum curator. A patron discovered them and he and the curator quietly called in an art expert to appraise them. But word got out and everyone wanted to own them. Or take them. The one on my parlor wall was hidden away, but someone stole the other two before the appraisal— and murdered the museum curator. Years later, after hearing the story, an associate of Theo's bid on his behalf for the remaining Benoit at a private auction and paid a hefty price for it.

"Theo told me this story when he presented the painting to me. But no one has ever found the two missing paintings, so some think that was just a hoax to bring attention to the one I own. But if there are two more paintings out there, they now have an estimated worth of over a million dollars each."

Gabriel did a low whistle. "So all three together…"

She let out a breath. "Could be worth close to three or four million at the least." She did the hand-to-the-chin pose. "Theo often talked about finding the other two. He even described them, based on some research he'd found on some old catalog notes from the original museum. And now that I think about it, the smaller rendition found on the balcony fits one of the descriptions he told me about. That's why it seemed so familiar."

Gabriel was beginning to see the whole picture. "And if someone has the other two and wants the one here, they could make a pretty penny on re-sale alone. Or possibly, they don't have any of the paintings, but think you have all three. Either way, if they get their hands on all three, they could become wealthy in a big way. They'd sell cheap, however, to stay under the radar. The price wouldn't be in the millions, but they could quite possibly ask for an easy three-hundred K."

"But I don't have the other two."

Gabriel put his hands on her arms. "No, but they might be after the one you do have in order to own the whole set. And they might be trying to scare you away long enough to get in here and take it."

"Or kill me and do whatever they want with all the art I've collected for the fundraiser."

"How many pieces are planned for the upcoming reception and silent auction?"

She tilted her head. "The Benoit—that's the main attraction, but of course, it's for display only. Two sculpture pieces worth several thousand dollars and one of Esther's that has been rising in value since her notoriety with the Levi-Lafitte Diamond and two more smaller paintings—a Van Gogh sketch and one of a Tahitian landscape, both valued at a quarter of a million."

"Where are they stored?"

She gave him a thoughtful look, as if she was sizing him up. "In a Mardi Gras Krewe warehouse over in Algiers. But no one except my immediate staff knows that. They will be transported to the auction venue on the day of the event."

"Which is?"

"Two weeks from now."

"And you obviously have an alarm system to protect these masterpieces?"

"Of course. We have one at the warehouse and one here. It's very discreet, but we had that installed when we moved in, after Theo gave me the Benoit. He also brought over some of his own treasured pieces. Between that and the guards, and now the police, I should think the Benoit is safe here until we get ready to move it. The sensor will go off if anyone dares touch the painting."

"Nothing is ever really safe, Princess. Not when it involves money."

"Not even me?"

"Especially not even you. You might be more valuable than you realize." Dead or alive, he thought to himself.

She tilted her head again. "I'm only as valuable as the next public appearance or fundraiser.

And now apparently because of my penchant for fine art."

He stared down at her, amazed at how calm she seemed. "I think you should call off the fundraiser gala."

"No," she said. "I won't allow whoever this is to scare me away. I'll tell Malcolm to put extra security at the warehouse and here. Making money on art is one thing, but leaving this city in need is not on my agenda."

"Even if your life is threatened?"

"I have security, and if this is the case, they will be alert and ready. Malcolm will bring in more people at the actual event, of course."

Gabriel didn't want to add to her burden, but he had to ask. "And what if someone close to you is in on this? Most art crimes occur because of an inside informant, someone who helps the thieves, makes things easy for them."

She shook her head, but Gabriel caught a hint of apprehension in her eyes. "The Benoit is still here, and if anyone touches it, alarms will go off everywhere. I'm safe for now. I trust my entire team."

"But that man last night made it all the way to an upstairs balcony. And no one heard or saw him until he'd almost entered the house."

"Deidre is a light sleeper, thankfully."

"What woke her?"

"She said she heard a noise out on the balcony. I'm sure the authorities have grilled her thoroughly.

The poor girl was scared and confused, but she can't go back to bed until they clear out of her room."

"And you can't be safe here. You need to think about that."

Her eyes took on that princess mode. "As I told you, the Benoit will be protected and so will I. I won't run from these people. I intend to see this through."

Gabriel wondered about that and the staunch determination in her eyes. He turned to see what Deidre was doing, but the woman, usually so bustling and hyper he could hear her coming a mile away, had slipped unnoticed out of the kitchen. "You need to be completely sure about that, Princess."

An hour later, Lara stood staring up at the Benoit, her thoughts a jumble of confusion that made her appreciate the dream aspects of the painting. Or rather, the lost dream that seemed to hang like a veiled curtain over the smiling, dancing people in the center.

When would her life ever settle down to a routine that might bring her a bit of contentment and harmony? After the gala, she reminded herself, her nerves jingling their own warning. The Benoit was the draw. Or at least she was counting on that.

Her cell rang. "Hello?"

A deep breathing. Well, that was original.

"Hello?" she repeated.

The connection went cold. And so did her heart.

Him again? Did he think he'd win her over by breathing into the phone?

"Another wrong number?"

She whirled to find Gabriel standing just inside the door.

"You startled me. I thought you were with Malcolm."

"We finished our discussion and I was allowed to get a couple of shots of the print you found. I didn't mean to startle you." He advanced into the room and brought the scents of spice and fresh soap with him. "If you're receiving hang-up calls, you need to let Malcolm and the police know."

She nodded, put her phone away, pushed her fears aside. "And you are here to watch and observe, not give me security advice."

"I'm sorry again." He glanced up at the painting. "But you're right, of course."

Lara shook her head. "Forgive me. I'm a little rattled. But I have to take this seriously since my entire staff could be in danger. I'd rather lose this painting than have something terrible happen to the people I love."

"But you're not willing to cancel this whole event?"

"I can't at this late date. Too many variables." And she didn't know him well enough to explain those variables.

He came to stand beside her, and Lara immediately felt the warmth descending over her like a cloak of protection. "And the people who love you don't want anything bad to happen to their princess."

She turned, surprised at the generosity in that statement. "I thought you were cynical about such things."

His smile was almost sad. "You guessed that about me already?"

"I read up on you. You've seen the worst the world has to offer, so I can certainly understand being cynical."

He glanced at the painting, then back to her. "Ah, but I've also seen the best the world has to offer. So in spite of being somewhat cynical, I also have a strong sense of faith."

"Really?" Lara was touched and surprised by his admission. "I'm relieved to hear that. My faith has guided me through the worst of times, too."

He turned, his gaze solemn and full of secrets. "You'll need that in the coming months, too. My gut tells me that these people trying to scare you are just getting started." Then he leaned close, his hand touching her wrist. "And I've come to a decision about that."

Lara held her breath while she watched the rich liquid brown of his eyes turn deadly serious. "You're not backing out of your assignment, are you? I didn't mean to be so rude—"

He got even closer, his mouth so close to her ear she felt her teardrop pearl earring dancing. "Oh, no, Princess, I've decided even though this is none of my business I'm staying close by your side until we find out who's doing this."

Lara swallowed her fear and shock. "You don't need to—I mean, that's not necessary. I have protection."

"I'm not a security expert, but I'm good at observing people and I know human nature. I'll be watching for anyone out of the ordinary."

She glanced over at him then. "Are you implying that you truly believe what you stated earlier? That someone on my security detail or within my household could be involved in this?"

He whirled her around to face him. "I'm not implying, Lara. I'm pretty sure that Deidre planted both of those packages. Your assistant is trying to terrorize you. And me, being the curious-reporter type, well, I intend to catch her in the act next time she makes a move. That is, if I can find her."

Lara wanted to slap him, but the dead-serious look in his dark eyes told her this was no joke. "You only came into my house last night and now you insult me by even suggesting such a thing as Deidre being involved?"

His next words sent a chill through Lara's heart. "I just checked her room. Now that the police have left and your detail people are back at their duties, I wanted to talk to her alone."

"And?"

"She's not there and neither is her laptop or her tote bag. I checked her closet, too. It's empty. Deidre has apparently left Kincade House."

FOUR

Lara couldn't believe this man's audacity. She'd only met him last night and already he was bossing everyone around. Normally, she liked forceful personalities. But today had not been normal. "You snooped in Deidre's room? Do you want me to end this assignment for you before we even begin?"

Gabriel checked the room, his expression full of concern and regret. "Look, Princess, I get these hunches about things."

"So you just go on a hunch and assume that my assistant is involved in an attempted art theft?"

He held his hands on his hips. "I go on what I see, on things I can put together and figure out." Tapping his temple with a finger, he added, "It's called logic."

Lara didn't want to listen to him and the rebel in her fought against his logic. He'd waltzed in here like Mr. America, all gung ho and alpha male, and now he was acting like the CIA? Never mind that his words and his sincere determination made shivers of apprehension move down her scalp. Never mind that his presence here made everything different and difficult. What had she been thinking, allowing him to shadow her at a time when she needed a lot of privacy?

"You are in no position to assume that authority, Mr. Murdock. Do I need to call Malcolm in here to escort you out?"

"Is there a problem, Your Highness?"

They both whirled at the sound of Deidre's voice.

Lara was as surprised as Gabriel. "Deidre, we were concerned about you. Where on earth did you go?"

She sent an accusing glare at Gabriel, then stepped toward her frazzled assistant. But when she came around the sofa, she saw Deidre's suitcase near her sandaled feet.

Gabriel was right behind her. This time he gave her a telling stare. Obviously, he thought he was right.

But she knew he was wrong.

"Deidre, what's going on?" Lara asked, wondering if she'd finally given in to that nervous breakdown the tabloids always claimed she was about to have.

Deidre started crying. "I wanted to leave, ma'am. I wanted to get out of this city."

"And why would you want to do that?" Lara asked, another shiver going down her spine.

"I've made a mess of things," Deidre replied. "I

was almost to the corner, but Malcolm came and got me and forced me to return. He said even if you wanted me to leave, I couldn't now. I'd compromise the…investigation."

"The investigation?" Lara gave Gabriel a blaming glance, then went to Deidre. "Sit down and tell me what you mean."

"Mr. Malcolm said there was a criminal investigation, since you've received two odd packages. He said it's not safe to leave now. He told me if I left, I'd look guilty."

"He's correct," Gabriel said, his eyes full of apology. "Deidre, it's none of my business, but if you know something that can help you or the princess, you need to tell us now."

"I don't," Deidre replied, pushing her dark glasses up on her nose, her gaze darting from Lara back to him. "I only know that I saw a man on the upstairs balcony last night. I didn't even see the package."

"That's true," Lara said, deciding she'd deal with Gabriel Murdock later. "I'm the one who alerted Malcolm and his team about the package."

Deidre stopped sobbing and stilled, shock coloring her face. "You don't think that I—"

"Of course not," Lara replied, taking Deidre by the hand. She lifted her gaze toward Gabriel, daring him to voice what she knew he must be thinking. "But…Deidre, Mr. Murdock does have a point. Since no one witnessed the first delivery and Herbert is not answering his phone to verify what you told us last night and now you claim you saw a man—"

"I did see a man," Deidre said, getting up to whirl around. "I don't know anything else. I brought you the first package, but I found it. I didn't plant it, if that's what you're implying. That's the truth. I'd never do anything to harm you."

Gabriel lifted his chin toward Lara. "May I say something else?"

Lara wanted to tell him no. She wanted to tell him to leave her house. But that little niggle of reality kept her from sending Gabriel away. That and the concern in his dark eyes.

"What?"

He gave her a nod of thanks. "Deidre, I'm the one who suspected you. Princess Lara was concerned for you, but I suggested that you might be involved. I apologize. It was very brave of you to come back and face her."

"She's brave because she has nothing to hide, right, Deidre?" Lara was determined to make him see that he was wrong. If she couldn't trust Deidre, whom could she trust?

"I'm telling the truth," Deidre replied. "Truly, ma'am, I wouldn't do anything to hurt you."

"We believe you, don't we, Gabriel?"

He stared at her a long minute before nodding. "I don't want to get involved in this, but I'm here and it's hard to avoid. It's the nature of being an investigative photojournalist. Too curious for my own good."

Deidre's dark gaze probed him. Then she turned to Lara. "May I please go to my room now? I'll unpack and we can finish what's left of today's schedule."

Lara got up and hugged Deidre. "You go, but don't worry about today's schedule. Take a long nap. I'll make sure Malcolm posts a guard by your door."

Deidre nodded and grabbed her small suitcase. Lara waited until she heard the girl's footsteps on the stairs. She turned to Gabriel, but Malcolm popped in the door.

"Ma'am, I hope the girl explained her absence and her return."

Lara nodded. "She did, Malcolm. Thank you for going after her."

He nodded, then left as silently as he'd come. Odd that Malcolm hadn't even questioned her acceptance of Deidre's return. Usually, the man was full of questions. But then, this whole affair had taken on a strangeness that didn't set well with Lara. Not a good way to start out her time here in New Orleans.

Lara took a deep, settling breath. "And as for you, Gabriel Murdock—"

Gabriel moved toward her like a panther stalking a dove. "You can't be serious. Do you actually believe her?"

"Yes, I certainly do. She's young and afraid and confused. I believe she got scared out of her wits and wanted to go home to her family in Europe. Sometimes, we all just want to go home."

He stared down at her and nodded, his expression changing to something less forceful. "Am I still on this assignment, Princess?"

She thought about that long and hard, and then she nodded. "Of course. We're all a little fatigued and on edge. I appreciate you being so diligent, but you need to remember you are not here to do any investigative journalism. You're only here to do an in-depth study on me. A factual, enlightening study to showcase my work here in New Orleans. Do I make myself clear?"

He leaned close, the scent of something spicy and masculine surrounding him. "Very clear, Princess. I'll report what I see and I'll write what I know to be true. But you have to know—this threat is not over." He hesitated, then rushed ahead. "And you also have to know that I won't stand by and watch if I think something is about to happen to you."

She grabbed at her pearls and inclined her head, hoping to distract herself from the way this man seemed to have a natural need to protect her. Maybe that was just the way he was wired, but his actions were somewhat confusing. "We're all aware now. We'll watch and wait, and I'm sure between Malcolm and the police, this will soon end."

He moved toward his equipment bags. "Then let's get started with your day."

Lara cleared her mind and tried to focus on the many tasks at hand. But she couldn't get past Gabriel's suggestion that Deidre wasn't being honest.

Especially when she'd noticed how strange her assistant had been acting lately. Was Deidre scared because of all the unsettling things happening around here? Or did the other woman actually know who was behind this?

Gabriel took another shot, from a different angle. The afternoon sun glistened off of Lake Pontchartrain and cast a golden shimmer around the woman in the stark white sundress.

Lara Kincade was in PR mode. This press conference would announce her intentions of building more Kincade houses in one of the disaster-stricken wards of New Orleans. With the lake behind her and most of the Louisiana press before her, Lara commanded the mike space with a regal elegance.

He wanted to capture that elegance.

So he snapped away with two different cameras and several lenses. He caught her smiling softly. He captured her with a hand lifted in the air, her diamond solitaire a signal that while she might be alone, she still held her marriage as sacred.

"And so, I'm happy to announce that I have a team of contractors and carpenters on standby to finish the work my husband started. I'm very excited and blessed to be able to be a part of this important recovery phase for the city of New Orleans."

After a round of applause, Deidre—wide-awake and back in control—stepped to the mike. "And now Her Royal Highness will be happy to take your questions."

Everyone started talking at once. Out of habit, Gabriel turned to snap a few pictures of the crowd. It never hurt to record anything that might become history. It never hurt to get faces that might become assets or foes later, either.

Or in this case, help him to protect the princess even more—the princess who didn't want to be protected. The woman was a walking target, but she had a job to do. He had to admire her fortitude. But he was also grateful for Malcolm and his expert security team. And having pictures of the crowd could serve as backup later. If anything else happened.

Gabriel had a feeling something else would happen. And soon. With art worth millions hanging around, and a highly visible princess taking up residence in the city, New Orleans was abuzz with intent. Some of it good and some of it bad.

He watched Deidre, too. The girl who'd been so rattled this morning now seemed as polished and cultured as a fresh pearl. Not the same girl who'd cried and played coy earlier. She'd appeared after lunch and just in time for the press conference that Lara had refused to cancel. What was the story with that one, anyway? He could always do a background check on her later, on his own time.

But right now he had to keep at the subject at hand.

He snapped away, his methods unobtrusive, and managed to get some candid shots of both the princess and Deidre.

"How long do you plan to be in New Orleans, Princess Lara?"

"As long as it takes."

"Are you staying in the Garden District?"

"I'm here and there."

"Why do you think it's so important to rebuild houses here?"

"Why wouldn't it be important? We can't have a fabulous city without people to contribute. And we can't bring people back unless they have houses in which to live."

"What about the Benoit?"

That caught Gabriel's attention. He whirled to see who'd asked that question. Snapping away, he caught the man's image in his pictures. Then he turned back to the princess. And saw her skin had gone pale.

"What *about* the Benoit?"

"We hear you're having a gala in the Quarter, a private affair with a very high ticket price. Is that because you want to show off the Benoit?"

"I hope to have a nice evening with invited guests. It's not about showing off. We picked that venue because it allows us to spill out into Jackson Square and it has a nice garden out back. But this event is about raising more money to help our cause."

The man nodded but looked skeptical and a bit angry.

Bingo. Gabriel's gut churned and he stopped taking pictures so he could study the reporter who'd asked that question. The man looked to be in his mid-thirties, with dark, straight hair and stark, almost black eyes. Was he really a reporter? Or a plant? Part of a team?

Gabriel would have to get his editor to access face-recognition technology and run a search online to find out about the man's credentials. And he could certainly enlarge the picture he'd snapped to see what the man's press badge said.

"Thank you all for your time," Lara said, clearly tired and a bit unnerved by the mention of the Benoit. "I so appreciate all of you coming today. But we have a very busy schedule."

Only Reporter Man wasn't finished. "What about the trouble at your Garden District home this morning?"

Lara looked shocked, but she lifted that noble chin and stared the man down. "I have no further comments."

Deidre stepped up to give instructions on where and when the construction would start. They'd need the press there to make sure they got even more coverage. But they would not be answering any more questions right now. Before she left the stage, the girl glared at the intrusive reporter.

Lara stepped down from the podium and met Gabriel behind the portable stage. "Don't even say it," she whispered as she moved by him.

He hurried to catch up with her. "Say what?"

"You know exactly what." She waited for the driver to open the door of the sleek black SUV. "That man asked about the Benoit. And he knows something is going on, obviously."

"Yes." Gabriel slid in beside her while Deidre got up front with the driver. "So?"

Lara gave him a quizzical glance. "I guess you wouldn't know."

"Know what?" Gabriel waited, wondering what else he didn't know.

"I haven't mentioned the Benoit to anyone. The press, I mean. The gala reception is supposed to be a private event and we haven't published it a lot. Only the people on the guest list know that the Benoit will be on display during the party."

Gabriel sat up. "Hmm. Now that does make things interesting. So how did that reporter know about the painting being back at Kincade House?"

"I have no idea," she replied, her voice low. "But this does give me pause."

"Good. You need to pause and think about the danger of this situation."

"I've thought about that a lot, I can assure you.

If I stayed hidden from danger, I'd never leave my bedroom."

Gabriel could understand her need to keep working, to keep moving. He'd been on his own so long, he'd learned to never be afraid of anything, but right now he had a deep dread inside his heart. "So you'll allow that something odd is going on. Someone is leaking information, Princess."

He glanced up front. The driver headed across town and exited off one of the main thoroughfares. Deidre had her nose buried in her smartphone, her thumbs tapping, tapping some sort of message.

Lara's gaze followed his. "Would you like to stay for dinner again tonight, Mr. Murdock?"

Gabriel couldn't miss an opportunity to take more pictures and to keep a close eye on the princess. This mystery was growing by the minute. In spite of his better judgment, he had to find out what was going on. He had a story here. A real story. He'd walked away before and that had put him here. It was like déjà vu all over again.

He shot a glance toward the front. "I'd love that."

"Good." She looked up again. "I think we have a lot to discuss."

He nodded, and wondered if the princess had finally seen the light and come to her senses. If so, maybe he could sit back and relax a little bit.

But in the next second, that notion changed. A boom hit the dusk and the SUV started spinning out of control.

"Tire just blew out," the driver shouted. Deidre screamed and dropped her phone.

Gabriel grabbed Lara, his eyes locked with hers. "Hold on," he said, pushing her down against the seat.

The impact of the crash set them both up and back down.

He was still holding Lara when the vehicle finally stopped spinning.

FIVE

The silence stretched for a few seconds; then everyone starting talking at once.

Deidre's sob echoed over the driver's shouts.

"Everyone okay?" the dazed man kept shouting.

"Good. I think we're good," Gabriel said, hoping that was the truth. He searched Lara's face, his nose inches from hers. "Are you all right?"

She nodded, gulped a breath. "Yes, thank you."

The rush of adrenaline tapered off while he studied her big, frightened eyes. Ignoring Deidre's screams and the driver's foul language, he asked, "Are you sure?"

He didn't mind holding her in his arms, but he was worried that she'd been injured. Checking closely for blood or bruises, he swept her hair away from her eyes.

"If you'll please let me up—"

Gabriel sat up and lifted her, his gaze following her every move. "Any pain? Cuts, bruises?"

"I only hit my head, but I think I'm okay."

Gabriel went into action then. "Driver, are you all right?"

The man nodded, but Gabriel saw a trace of blood slipping down the man's face. "You need a doctor."

Before he could check on Deidre, Lara pushed past him to touch the girl on her arm. "Deidre, how are you doing?"

"I'm fine," Deidre said, crying again. "Just a little wobbly, ma'am."

"I'll call for help." Gabriel opened the door and stared out onto the busy exit ramp. While he explained their location to the 911 operator, he noticed they'd left the freeway and landed on a side street that would take them back to the Garden District. The SUV had rolled up an embankment, probably due to the driver's expertise. If the tire had blown when they'd been up on the busy thoroughfare, things could have been a lot worse. They might have plunged off the main artery and hit this road head-on.

The princess might have died.

His heart hammered a skittish warning beat that repeated *not again, not again, not again.* After checking on everyone once more, he found some water and gave it to Lara.

"Drink this," he gently urged, his eyes locking with hers.

"It's been a rather exciting day," she said, her tone

shaky but light. "And I told you nothing exciting ever happened to me."

"You're nothing *but* exciting," he replied, very much aware that she was close to having a hissy fit. He hoped she didn't go into shock.

But then, this was Her Royal Highness Lara Kincade. She took a dainty sip of the bottle of water, cleared her expression, touched a hand to her hair and then gave him a challenging glance. "May I please exit the vehicle? I need some air."

Gabriel stepped back, did a visual of the area and then nodded. "Stay near me, please."

She did the chin-lift thing. "Deidre, are you sure you're okay?"

"Yes, ma'am." Deidre stayed in her seat, her head down. Every now and then Gabriel heard a sniffle. He handed her a bottle of water, too. But she just held it tightly in her hand.

"I can't find my phone."

"I'll look for it," the driver said. That busied him and kept Deidre focused.

And gave Gabriel a chance to whisper in Lara's ear. "I don't think this was an accident."

She didn't even flinch. "Neither do I."

Gabriel kept checking the noisy highway above them and the streets surrounding them. "They could be watching right now."

"I'm aware of that, too."

"What do you want to do next?"

"Right now I want to go home and have a private fit."

He smiled in spite of his jangled nerve endings. "What exactly happens when you have a private fit?"

She shook her head, gave him a defiant glare. "I mostly pace and throw pillows. If I actually throw plates or vases, someone will come running. I wish just once I could throw a whole set of china and not have anyone be concerned about it."

He turned serious again. "Are you going to be all right for now?"

She got serious right back. "Do I have a choice?"

Sirens wailed down the ramp. "The cavalry has arrived," Gabriel said. "Let the paramedics give you a good examination, Lara."

"Of course." But that defiant chin challenged the notion.

"I'm serious." He did another scan of her face and her clothes. She looked as lovely as ever in her pastel flared dress and pearls. "How do you do it?"

Eyeing the EMTs, she asked, "Do what?"

"Stay so calm."

"I'm not that calm," she said on a catchy breath. "I'm so practiced in staying calm, always holding up my head, that my heart has forgotten how to feel anything, I think."

Her eyes turned a rich blue-green. The glance she gave him was washed in regret and longing, in anticipation and apprehension. She sure was feeling something right now.

And Gabriel felt it right back. An awareness, a stirring, a need to…hold tight.

He let her go. Now was not the time to explore these odd and fascinating tingles and jangles moving throughout his system. Now was not the time to remind himself that this woman was so over his pay grade.

But someone, somehow, had to make the princess see that she was in danger.

Gabriel had seen enough death and destruction to know all the signs. Someone wanted the princess out of New Orleans.

Or worse…dead.

"Another quiet night at home."

Lara turned from the Benoit to give Gabriel an elegant frown. "Hello, Gabriel. I'm sorry about the accident yesterday, but I hope you got some rest last night."

"I did all right. How about you?"

"I didn't sleep very well, but I'm a light sleeper on a good day. I'm a bit sore, but I'll be okay." She did a shoulder roll to hide her nervousness. "You had to come to my rescue yet again. I don't think that's what you signed on for, and I'd rather you didn't put all this nastiness in the photo essay."

"I don't mind helping out, and I don't mind leaving all of this out of my story," Gabriel replied. "But

I do mind that you refuse to cancel your upcoming public appearances and the big event coming up."

"We've been over this," Lara said, exhaustion tugging at her from every direction. "I've been planning this event for close to a year now. I can't cancel the gala. I have dignitaries coming from the state and the city, and some coming from Washington and Europe, too. I've made a pledge to give the ticket money to the Kincade House foundation. I can't go back on my word now, and I need you to cover the affair to reassure your readers that I'm doing what my husband wanted to do."

He got up off the couch and came to stand next to her. "Even if someone is trying to kill you?"

Lara ignored the shivers hitting her skin like needles. "We don't have proof of that."

"Yet," he added. "But I'm going to find that proof. I didn't come here for this, but I won't stand by and watch you get hurt or worse."

He sounded confident and dangerous, but Lara refused to let him put himself in any more danger. She'd started this, so she'd be the one to finish it. "That's not your job."

"It is now."

Lara tried to ignore the way his eyes washed over her with a dark concern. She was terrified that he might be right about the odd happenings around here, but she'd learned a long time ago to hide her fears. She'd also learned she couldn't trust people. She'd been naive once but not anymore. "I have people looking into this, Gabriel. Malcolm and the police are going over the SUV to see what could have happened."

"And I don't trust those people or the police, either, right now. In spite of the tight security around you, someone has breached your home twice and managed to damage one of the tires on your vehicle, too."

Lara came up with excuses to convince herself. "We don't have proof that someone tampered with the tire. That's why Malcolm is investigating the accident."

"But earlier, you agreed that we didn't think this was an accident."

She nodded, played with her pearls. "Yes. But I want to wait for Malcolm's report before I give in to that conclusion."

His frown darkened. "Why are you so stubborn?"

She continued to play with her necklace. "Why are you so suspicious?"

"Can't you see what's happening right in front of your eyes?"

"I can see plenty," she retorted, her arms pressing against the linen of her dress. "But I can't let *them* see that I'm afraid. I've been through this before, many times. For some reason, if you have money and a title, some people seem to resent everything you do. So they make threats and try to frighten you away. I'm not that easily frightened. I came here with a purpose and I intend to see that purpose to fruition. As long as my detail team stays alert, I should be safe."

Gabriel touched his hands to her arms. "But what if your team can't stay on top of this?"

"They will."

"I don't believe that. Something new happens every day, and this is only the first week I've been with you."

She gave him a direct stare. "You're on Malcolm's watch list, you know. This did start when you arrived."

"Are you serious?"

"Of course. Don't disregard my team, Gabriel."

"Don't disregard my warnings, Princess."

Lara couldn't deny he had a point, but she had her reasons for refusing to cancel the gala. "What do you think I should do? Run away? I was taught to never give up, to never quit."

"You wouldn't be giving up, Lara. You'd just have to adjust your plans."

She gave him a long, intrigued stare. "What do you mean?"

"They must have your schedule or eyes on you so they can find out your schedule. I suggest you rearrange everything, starting today, without telling anyone, including Deidre, what your next move is going to be. That way, you can take care of business, but they won't be one step ahead of you. We need to throw them off." He shrugged, glanced toward the open pocket doors to the entryway. "Unless, of course, you have a mole on your team."

"Are we back to that?"

"I never left that. You need to consider every possibility."

Hoping to distract him, she turned and grabbed her briefcase. She didn't want him to see the doubt in her eyes. Or the deception. "Right now I have a meeting with the auction curator. Are you coming?"

"You better believe it." He grabbed his equipment and his many cameras. "I'll be waiting with Malcolm out by the garage."

Lara let out a sigh of relief. If she stayed focused on her purpose, this would be over soon. In the meantime, she also needed to keep Gabriel busy so he'd stop being an amateur sleuth.

Later that day, Lara glanced toward the dining room, where they'd just shared a meal Deidre had made. "I'm worried about Herbert. He always stays here in the house when I'm in town. But no one has heard from him since he finished cooking the other night. Not one word in three days."

Gabriel nodded, checked his watch. "Even you have to admit that's suspicious."

Outside, the golden-pink dusk filtered through the mossy oaks and swaying palm trees. Night was coming. What would happen next? As much as she loved New Orleans, the city now held a sinister darkness that kept her on edge. But she couldn't reveal her feelings to anyone right now. She wanted this over with and done. Starting to wonder at her own sanity, Lara reminded herself she had a goal and a plan to reach that goal.

Going back to Gabriel's observation, she said, "Yes, it is. I got so busy and then with everything else that happened yesterday, I neglected to talk to Malcolm about that. Herbert is known for going off on weekends, but he always comes back. The police don't think he's a priority." She whirled, her full-skirted dress twirling around her. "Better yet, I can go and check on him myself."

"Oh, no." Gabriel followed her to the hallway. "Not a good idea, Princess."

She turned and leaned up, so he would hear every word. "But if I'm to trust no one, then I must find out for myself, don't you think?"

A couple of silent seconds ticked by.

"Oh. No. No way. I refuse to go with you."

Lara knew she was playing with fire, but she had to make sure Herbert was safe since the police seemed so nonchalant about his comings and goings. They'd questioned the entire household after the second intruder, but the locals hadn't found anything to confirm that Herbert was missing, and they couldn't connect him to the intruders at this point. But she could at least check his apartment. She'd often managed to sneak out for some girl time with her friends when she was first married, but those days seemed like a lifetime ago. She didn't know Gabriel very well, but he was her best hope right now.

This is not a shopping trip, she reminded herself. *This could get you in a lot of trouble.*

She eyed him now. "You're right. Silly idea."

He turned to leave, stomped back. "You're going without me, aren't you?"

She lifted on her tiptoes to check the room. "I have to know. I'm worried and Malcolm will throw a fit if I ask him to do this."

Gabriel rubbed his hand down his face, stared at the floor, then finally lifted his head. "I don't like this at all, but I won't let you go alone. And of course, you know that."

Lara had hoped that, but she let out a sigh of relief, all the same. "Thank you. I'll take full responsibility. But how can we get away?"

"I have ways of shaking off a detail."

Lara wondered when and why she'd decided to trust this man. But after spending the day with him shadowing her like an unobtrusive knight, she'd seen the professional side of Gabriel Murdock. And she was impressed. He took pictures, lots of them, in a rapid session that never intruded. He took notes on a small pocket notebook, scribbling so silently, she forgot he was there. She had no doubt he could handle just about any situation. She needed someone like Gabriel Murdock in her corner.

"I can only imagine. After all, you are a reporter of sorts. You'd like to get the scoop on what's really happening here, right?"

"Absolutely." He walked her back to the parlor. "I've never tried to hide that. But I am professional and I won't break the promise I made to you. This only goes public if you give me the word, but I'd be crazy to ignore the things happening to you. Until then, the only thing people will see in my pictures and story is the truth—that you're here to do good work and to help the city of New Orleans." He went silent, his eyes still following her. "That is the truth, isn't it?"

Lara's heart skipped ahead a couple of beats. He couldn't find out the whole story. His eyes, so intense and so sincere, scared her. And intrigued her. She wanted to know his background, to understand why he chased stories and took pictures of both beauty and horror. She should tell him she'd changed her mind about finding Herbert, but she couldn't bring herself to do that. Herbert had helped her with certain aspects of this whole affair. Had she put the jovial chef in danger?

"Yes, that is the truth." Now she felt really awful because that was only part of the truth. She didn't want to involve him in the rest.

"Okay." He seemed pacified with her declaration. "Will you go with me, then?"

"Do you know where Herbert lives?"

"Yes. He sometimes stays across the river in Algiers."

"Then let's go." He pulled her close. "But you have to do exactly as I say. Malcolm will be furious with us, and I don't want to get shot."

"I have a gun."

"No!" He shook his head, his words a low growl. "We do this my way, Princess, or no way at all."

That demand made her wary. "What if you're the mole? What if you're trying to lure me away from the people I pay to protect me?"

Gabriel's gruff chuckle sent chills up her bare arms. "Seriously, you want to go back over that again? Do you think I'd leave those packages or set foot in a vehicle I purposely sabotaged?"

"You did accuse poor Deidre and you had the means and opportunity to leave those packages, same as she did. Maybe you knew the blown tire wouldn't cause a serious accident."

"You don't believe that, do you?"

Lara couldn't picture this man trying to scare her or kill her. No, the only way she could picture Gabriel Murdock in her mind involved him holding her close and whispering to her, the way he'd done several times in their brief time together.

Pushing that image away, Lara shook her head. "I don't think you're behind this. But I have to be able to trust you, Gabriel. Don't sell me out, to the press or to anyone's greed."

"I gave you my word," he replied. "Now, are we doing this or not? I have pictures to download and some captions to edit."

"We are," she whispered. "But how?"

He leaned close again. "Remember, do exactly as I say and I'll have you gone and back before Malcolm can sneeze. If we find something wrong at Herbert's place, we'll call Malcolm and the police."

"All right. I'll go change."

"Wear black," he advised. Then his gaze swept down her legs. "And…take off those heels."

SIX

"I feel like a cat burglar."

Gabriel glanced over at Lara with an appreciative grin. "A cute cat burglar." He parked the dark sedan a couple of blocks away from the address she'd given him earlier. "Am I allowed to say that to a princess?"

Lara's pulse leaped. But she couldn't be sure if it was from sneaking out without clearance or from sneaking out with this mysterious, interesting man. "You're allowed to say anything you want to me." She turned to glance around, noting the run-down buildings and old warehouses. "I'm beginning to doubt the wisdom of this nefarious adventure."

Gabriel shut off the engine and twisted toward her. "We are not doing anything evil or illegal. We're simply looking for your chef. Nobody else has bothered. The NOPD seems backlogged at best."

He was so logical. Nice trait. He'd managed to get her out of a guarded, security-tight house and into a taxi without anyone seeing them. They'd gone to his nearby apartment and were now in his car and across the river. Lara tried to block out her doubts and concerns. Herbert was probably off somewhere at a festival. Nothing to worry about at all.

"That is true," she said, watching for moving shadows in the muted streetlights. "So we have to at least check. Let's get on with it, then."

"Good idea. We can only fool Malcolm for a little while. He thinks you're sound asleep in your room."

Lara remembered the secret thrill of successfully getting past Malcolm's late-night guards. "Then we should have plenty of time. He has strict orders not to disturb me unless there is fire or blood."

"Well, you never know." Gabriel got out and came around to her side of the car. After opening the door, he said, "We've had some close calls."

"I'm so worried about Herbert." Her shuddering whisper seemed to echo down the dark, desolate street. "I've never known him to act this way. He's very dependable."

Gabriel's frown told her he thought the same, even if he didn't know Herbert. "All the more reason to find him and make sure he's not involved."

"I can't believe he would be involved in anything illegal or dangerous," she said. "Herbert is like a big teddy bear. Comfort food, not criminal activity, is his forte."

"I do find it strange that Malcolm and your team haven't tried to locate him."

"Malcolm had more pressing matters. He's focused on keeping me safe, and that sometimes narrows his awareness of other things."

She would have said more, but Gabriel already had a massive distrust of her security detail. She wouldn't add fuel to that fire yet. But Malcolm held a disdain for anyone he hadn't personally hired, so Herbert was a sore spot with him. Lara had insisted on bringing the chef into the fold. She prayed she wouldn't regret that decision.

They started walking toward the apartment building where Herbert supposedly lived. She was beginning to doubt that now, too. Her mother used to warn Lara about being too trusting, but she'd worked hard to hire the kind of people she thought she could trust. Especially on this particular mission in New Orleans.

She glanced over at Gabriel and hoped her instincts were right on this one. So far, so good. He was capable, handsome, dependable and…way too observant. But that came with his line of work, she supposed. She'd viewed some of his award-winning photo spreads, all in major magazines and newspapers, and lately exclusively with *RWN*. Gabriel knew how to capture the essence of a story in his images. That was one of the reasons she'd agreed to let him tag along with her.

But she'd never dreamed they'd go out on a clandestine assignment such as this.

Gabriel checked the address she'd written on a

business card. "Okay, his is Unit 1102. Let's see if we find him."

Lara searched the dark buildings. After her earlier bravado, she now realized she wasn't used to being out in the world without a security team around her. Maybe she shouldn't have been so impulsive.

"Are you all right?" Gabriel asked, his hand on her arm.

"Yes. Just nervous. I don't often go out dressed like a ninja."

He shot her a quick smile. "We'll be in and out and back home in no time." Guiding her with a gentle hand against her back, he added, "Herbert is probably sleeping away and unaware we're worried."

He said. She hoped. "Okay, let's just do this and get out of here."

Gabriel knocked softly on the wooden door. Now that Lara's eyes had adjusted to the dark, relief overtook some of her apprehension. This wasn't such a bad apartment complex, after all. Bougainvillea and morning-glory vines trailed along the covered walkways leading to each building. Tall magnolia trees shimmered darkly in the moonlight, and sago palms lifted in gentle sweeps between the buildings. She could smell the scent of jasmine. At least the flora and fauna were pleasant.

"No answer," Gabriel said. "I tried the doorbell, too."

"What now?" Lara asked, a shiver moving like

a floating leaf down her back. "He doesn't answer his cell. Maybe he did go out of town for a while."

"Let's go around back," Gabriel suggested, taking her hand to lead her through the trellised walkway.

They reached an enclosed patio, but when Gabriel tried the wooden gate, it fell open. "So he doesn't lock the gate."

"He's very thorough but also very friendly," Lara said by way of an explanation. "Probably too trusting, now that I think about it." *Just like me.*

Gabriel studied the rusty gate's latch for a few seconds, then stepped past old flowerpots and an ancient grill. After trying to see in a window, he touched the back door and turned the doorknob. "It's not locked," he said on a low whisper.

Lara's heartbeat shifted gears. She tried to ignore that and the chill bumps forming on her arms. "Should we go inside?"

Gabriel stood for a minute. "We can but...why don't you wait here?"

"No—oh, no. I am not going to wait here. I want to find Herbert."

Gabriel turned, his hands on her arms. "What if I find something you don't want to see?"

Putting a hand to her mouth, Lara gulped in a breath. "Do you think...?"

"I don't know. But he's been missing for over thirty-six hours and hasn't responded to our calls. The police haven't been able to question him, either, or haven't tried. Something isn't right." He held his cell to the door handle and clicked on a light. "Somebody tampered with this door, Lara." He glanced back behind her. "And I'm pretty sure the patio gate, too."

She stared down at the deep slashes in the wood around the doorknob and the door facing. "I can see that."

She did not have a good feeling about going in this apartment.

Gabriel held tight to her arm. "We have to find out, either way. I can go in and check."

"I'll be okay," she said, determined to find the truth. "Let's do it together. I promise I won't faint or scream."

His smile of appreciation warmed her heart, but the chills kept coming up her arms.

"Stay behind me," he said.

Lara didn't mind that command. She held tightly to his lightweight black jacket, using his broad shoulders as a shield against her fears.

The door made a creaking complaint when he pushed on it, the sound scratching and scraping like a scream until it went silent and still.

"It's jammed against something," Gabriel said over his shoulder. He squeezed his frame between the opening enough to shine the cell light down.

Suddenly the smell of jasmine disappeared to be replaced with another kind of smell. Lara gasped and stepped back.

Gabriel quickly shut the door. "We need to leave, right now."

Lara allowed him to tug her off the patio. She heard the gate slamming shut, but her mind couldn't move past that blocked door. "He's dead, isn't he?"

"Yes."

The one word echoed behind them with a solemn finality while their sneakers made tiny squeaking sounds against the graveled path.

"We have to call the police."

"Yes, we do. But first, I have to get you home."

She stopped, causing him to turn. "Gabriel, I can't... How are we going to handle this? I'm supposed to be asleep. How can I explain being here without the press going wild?"

"You will be asleep," he replied. "I'll tell the police I came to check on Herbert because you were concerned. I'll explain that I couldn't get him to come to the door."

That was true, but a bit stretched. Now she'd become part of a cover-up? Lara closed her eyes. "What have I done? What's happening?"

Gabriel pulled her into his arms, the warmth he brought calming the shivers moving through her. "We'll figure this out, Lara. We can't do anything for Herbert, but I can protect you."

She'd been in denial, of course. The same way she'd been in denial when her husband had died. Lara didn't want to believe what everyone told her. She couldn't imagine life without Theo so she couldn't believe he was dead. But he was gone and she'd learned a lot since then, things she didn't want to believe even now. Herbert was gone, too. And she had to believe he'd died because of the Benoit. And because of her.

Gabriel put away his cell phone and glanced up and down the street to make sure no one had seen them. He got Lara to the car and buckled her in, then stood and shut the passenger-side door. This was one sticky situation, and he blamed himself for bringing Lara here. He should have told her no and reported her to Malcolm. But Gabriel had been just as curious as Lara about the missing chef.

But he'd never thought they'd find Herbert dead. Gone, yes. But *gone* as in out of town or on the run. Too late for that now.

Herbert wouldn't be able to tell them anything. Gabriel had made the call to report what they'd found and he'd have to give a statement later, but right now he wanted to get Lara home. She hadn't seen the body, so she didn't need to comment.

A sound nearby alerted him before he made it around the car. He saw two men hurrying away from the complex, in the other direction from the way he and Lara had come. He watched as the men got into a car and sped away.

Herbert's killers? But no, the man had been dead for a while. Maybe someone was following them.

If he hadn't had Lara with him, Gabriel would have gone back to the apartment to get a feel for things. How long had Herbert been dead? Had those two men been watching the apartment and seen him and Lara trying to go inside?

Too many questions. Maybe the two men had been visiting someone else, but in his gut, Gabriel knew they or someone they worked for had killed the chef. Maybe they'd come back to get rid of the body or search the apartment. That, or they'd been waiting for someone to show up so they could question them, too.

He had to get Lara home. What had he been thinking, putting her in danger like this?

"I'm sorry," he told her after he cranked the car and pulled away from the complex. "I shouldn't have allowed you to do this."

"I insisted on coming," she said, sounding stronger now. "And now I know something terrible is going on around me. Herbert wouldn't have hurt a fly. He was gentle and jolly and loved to cook. Now he's gone. His life is over. It's not fair."

"No, it's not fair," Gabriel replied, his vision centered on the road, both before them and behind them.

The car he'd seen the two men enter zoomed up behind them. He recognized the flashy emblem on the front. Somebody had a lot of money. Obviously, they'd parked and waited so they could follow Gabriel.

"Lara, is your seat belt tight?"

She gave him a quizzical glance. "Of course. Why?"

"I think we're being followed. I saw two men back there, leaving the complex after we got to our car."

She let out another gasp and glanced around. "They're behind us now?"

"Pretty sure, yes." He shifted and changed lanes. The other car followed. "Hang on. I plan to lose them."

Gabriel sped up, hoping he could outrun the dark car behind him. But the driver only took that as a challenge. The other car came up on Gabriel's taillights, getting perilously close. One nudge and this vehicle could go spinning out of control.

Gabriel didn't mention any of his thoughts to Lara. She was worried enough as it was. "Just hold on. They might try something or they might just follow us."

"What if they shoot?"

"We'll duck."

"You're very funny."

"I don't have any other answer. I'm driving as fast as I can and I'm praying they don't shoot."

"Prayer. That is a good idea."

She closed her eyes, shutting them tight. Gabriel let her pray while he watched the car behind them.

When the car hurried toward them, he swerved to the other lane and barely missed being hit.

"Whoa," Lara said, grabbing the dash to steady herself. "At least the traffic isn't heavy."

"Yes, but I kind of wish it were. We could hide between cars."

"Sounds as if you've had experience with this sort of thing."

"I've had a few close calls, yes."

"Do you bring trouble with you wherever you go?"

"Can we discuss *me* later, Princess? Right now I'm trying to *avoid* trouble."

She quieted down but kept glancing back. "They're getting closer," she said. "But you're doing a good job of keeping us from being hit."

Gabriel wasn't so sure about that. One tap and it could all be over. He remembered another dark night a world away from here. And another woman who'd gotten caught in the cross fire. He switched lanes again, but the other car was ready this time. He saw headlights in the rearview mirror, then felt a slight shudder.

"They mean business," he shouted, holding tight to the wheel. Putting the past out of his mind, Gabriel was dead-set on not making the same mistake twice. He wouldn't let this woman get caught in the fray.

The other car zoomed close in the right lane, then swerved toward Lara's side of the car. She screamed and leaned away from the door. "They have guns, Gabriel."

Gabriel watched through the rearview mirror. "Get down."

He took off, but the other vehicle grazed the back fender of his car, causing him to shift and spin out. He heard a ping against the car metal. Bullets. Gabriel held to the wheel and righted the car, then glanced over at Lara.

"I'm okay," she said, her body slumped in the seat. "Just keep driving."

Gabriel gripped the steering wheel through several more assaults. Then he heard another gunshot. "Okay, now they're just showing off."

And he was getting mad. Why had he brought the princess out on a late-night recon trip anyway? He knew the danger, but he'd wanted her with him so he could protect her. And now he'd put her in even more danger. But at least she had to see that someone was after her. They'd left packages to terrorize her, they'd killed Herbert and they'd tried to kill her yesterday.

If this was about the Benoit hanging over her fireplace, someone must really want that painting badly. Or maybe they wanted the painting and also wanted the princess dead, too.

Either way, Gabriel was in this up to his eyeballs.

He had to protect Lara and he had to get her home safely.

The other vehicle skidded into the car again, hitting it over and over. Each bounce twisted through Gabriel like a knife; each crunch only reminded him that he was carrying precious cargo. He didn't dare let go of the wheel.

Just a little farther and maybe he could lose the other car. But when another shot rang out and shattered the back windshield, he had a bad feeling these guys wouldn't give up so easily. One more shot, one more crash against metal and he and the princess could both be dead.

He thought about the area and where they might hide. But when he looked up and saw the road, his heart hit triple time.

The only way back was across the Crescent Connection Bridge over the Mississippi.

It was now or never.

SEVEN

"Gabriel, the bridge! It's the only way across from this area."

They weren't near the water yet, but at this rate of speed they'd pass the land down below and be over the river soon.

Lara closed her eyes and prayed, wishing they'd taken the ferry. She could swim, but the Mississippi was known for its strong undercurrents. She'd never survive if the car plunged off the bridge. She'd probably pass out from fear before she ever hit that deep, dark water.

"I see the bridge," he said. "We're going over it, not off it, I promise."

He moved into the other lane. "I'll have to bypass the toll gate, but I think we'll be okay. Of course, they'll probably get a picture of my license plate."

Lara wasn't sure how the man could make such a promise, but she intended to hold him to that. "Gabriel?"

He reached out to her. "Take my hand."

"You have to drive the car," she replied, the sound of crunching metal grating against her ears. She wanted to grab his hand and hold on for dear life, but she held back.

The other car followed them and kept trying to hit their back bumper. If the driver got close enough to give them one good slam once they were on the bridge, they'd spin and hit the guardrail and could go plunging into the water.

"Give me your hand, Lara."

She took his hand, the feel of his fingers over hers giving her a warm comfort. This was all her fault. She prayed they'd get out of this alive.

The other car came up on them with a grinding speed, ramming against the car and pushing it close to the railing.

Gabriel squeezed her hand. "Listen to me. I'm going to try something and I hope it works. If it doesn't, we *will* go into the river."

"Gabriel, please—"

"Lara, listen to me. If we sail off this bridge, let your car window down. Can you do that?"

"I don't know," she shouted. "I've never had to try that trick."

"You have to open the window," he said. "Look, I'll open it a little way to get you started."

The feel of cool air hit her in the face, causing her to gulp. When another bullet pinged the car, she ducked down, her prayers caught inside her throat.

Gabriel let go of her hand and kept the car moving. She could see the toll gates and the beams of the bridge up ahead. His next words chilled her to the bone. "I'm going to do a one-eighty and ram them, hopefully near the HOV lane. If it works, we won't go into the water. But they should either jam against the rail or fall in the water."

Lara nodded. "If it doesn't work, I get to swim in the Mississippi River. We won't survive either way."

"Just do what you have to do," he shouted. "Lara, promise me. Our choices are hard concrete or the river."

"I promise." She wouldn't cry. She wouldn't panic. Her heart tried to escape her chest, but she took a deep breath, her finger on the window button. She could do this. Let the window down, exit the car and swim toward the shore. If the current didn't take her down and away.

Another jam, a few more bullets. And a bridge up ahead.

"Hold on," Gabriel said. "I'm going for it once we get past the toll gates. Let your window down as soon as we're clear, okay?"

Lara took another breath, said another silent prayer.

Gabriel accelerated enough to get a few feet ahead of the other vehicle. When they approached the toll, he sailed on through without a backward glance. The other car did the same. Gabriel pressed the gas again and gained some distance. Then he slammed his car to a fast stop and started going in reverse toward the other car.

"What are you doing?" Lara shouted.

"A spin," he replied, his head turned toward the rear, one arm over the seat.

He hit the other car with a bang, causing Lara's head to snap back. And he kept on pushing at the other car, still in reverse until they had backed out of the entry to the HOV lane. Traffic, which was light this time of night even in the other lanes, started coming to a stop. Horns honked, drivers screamed. Gabriel checked back and forth and kept pushing. Somehow, they managed to avoid hitting any other cars.

Lara caught vague details of stopped vehicles each time she looked out, but Gabriel didn't stop grinding or pushing at the other car. And then he shifted and sped away, then hit the brakes and turned the wheel, causing the car to spin around.

And land the way they'd been coming.

Lara's dizziness receded enough for her to catch her next breath. The long, lonely entrance to the HOV lane up ahead was empty now, except for the two cars going head-to-head on the entry ramp. The man in the passenger seat struggled to get off another shot. But Gabriel wasn't through. He was now facing the car he'd just bashed.

"Stay down and hold tight," he shouted.

The grinding of gears caused a smoking stink to hit Lara's nostrils. The whole car vibrated and shook in an angry rage, bullets now pelting them with each turn of the wheels.

She ventured a glance up and realized he was pushing the other car toward the drop-off over the banks of the Mississippi.

"Gabriel, be careful! They'll go over."

He didn't answer.

"Gabriel! Leave them and get us out of here!"

At first, Gabriel didn't let up. He kept pushing the other car closer and closer to the beginning spans of the bridge. Underneath, the road and green spaces changed to water. With a grunt and a determined look, he locked on to the other car and, with one final gunning of the gas pedal, stopped pushing just as the vehicle neared the low part of the guardrail.

The crash of the other vehicle hitting the concrete and steel railing sounded in Lara's ears, the grinding and the smoke, the smell of motor oil and gasoline, the honking traffic and...the sound of sirens somewhere in the distance.

Then the doors of the other car flew open and the two injured men took off back toward the west bank of the river.

"They're getting away," Lara shouted.

"Let them. We can't chase them now."

Gabriel let out a grunt of frustration, then let up on the gas and backed away. Silence filled the car. For a minute Gabriel sat there, his breath coming in quick gulps. Then he turned to her and took her into his arms. "We need to get you home before the police arrive."

"No, no," Lara said, her fingers moving through his tousled hair. "No, Gabriel. I'll give a statement. You were trying to save my life."

"But—"

"I can't run from this anymore," she said, her pulse pushing at her temple. "I'm in danger and that means everyone around me is in danger, too. If I go public about Herbert's death, that should send a warning to whoever is behind this."

"Or make you more of a target."

"I'm always a target."

They didn't have time to argue and she didn't have time to explain things to him right now. The first responders had arrived. Before Lara could say anything more, she was being prodded and probed and questioned by the bridge police and the NOPD. With so many witnesses with conflicting stories and with the press milling about with flashing cameras, it took a while to get the story straight. Gabriel showed his credentials, made a few calls and finally got the locals to understand that a man was dead and they had been under attack.

And that he was protecting a princess.

After she was escorted to a waiting ambulance, she turned toward Gabriel. He held up a hand and sent her an attempt at a reassuring smile.

Was he going to take the fall for her?

* * *

Two hours later, Gabriel and Lara arrived back at her home in the Garden District. They'd given statements to the police and to Malcolm. Gabriel had immediately called him to the scene, so Malcolm could vouch for them and help field questions from the growing crowd of reporters.

"They're camping out at my door again," Lara said, her voice scratchy and weary. "But at least now the word is out."

Gabriel checked her, saw the fatigue in her eyes. "You need to rest."

"I have obligations."

"No. You need to rest, really rest. I understand how important your obligations are to you, but a lot has happened since you arrived here a few days ago and you haven't had much sleep all week."

She stared out the darkened SUV glass at the dawn. The sun was cresting through the palm trees across from her home. "A lot has happened since I first came back here with Theo."

Gabriel could sense the defeat in her words even while he wondered what she meant. But he wasn't going to let these people win. He had a story now, and he intended to run with it. He'd managed to get a few pictures at the scene of the wreck. The car had jammed on the guard beam. The two men who'd chased them were still missing, but a BOLO had been issued based on Gabriel's description, and the locals were searching for the men. Gabriel wondered if they were somewhere hiding out or if they'd left New Orleans.

Would he ever know the truth of that?

His cell rang. He saw the name Richard Littleton on the caller ID. "My editor at the magazine," he said to Lara. "I'll call him back once we get you settled."

She didn't protest. She just stared out the window.

Malcolm pulled the sleek SUV up into the gated drive, ignoring the crowd of paparazzi hammering against the windows. Two guards made sure none of the reporters got inside the compound.

After they were safely in the backyard and underneath the open carport, Gabriel surveyed the area and hurried around the vehicle to help Lara out. She had already opened her door and stepped down, so he took her by the arm to guide her to the house.

But Malcolm stood blocking them. "I think you and I need to talk, Mr. Murdock. You broke every protocol we discussed last night and put the princess in danger." Turning to Lara, he said, "I think we should send Mr. Murdock packing, ma'am."

"I asked him to take me to find Herbert," she said, her head lifting, her back stiffening. "It was my idea to go without informing anyone, and he went along to protect me. He will remain for the duration of his assignment."

Malcolm's bushy eyebrows rose in disdain. "He

almost got you killed, and now the wolves are gathering to get the rest of this story."

"It's all right, Malcolm," she replied, the serenity of her words a stark contrast to the expression on her face. "I take full responsibility. Someone had to check on Herbert, and since neither you nor the police did so, I took matters into my own hands."

That shut up Malcolm. He moved aside, but kept his eyes on Gabriel.

"I could have stopped you," Gabriel said. "I *should* have stopped you."

"Enough!" She held up her right hand in dismissal. "I'm tired and heartsick. Herbert is dead and no one can explain to me why. I don't know if he was robbed at random or if his death is somehow connected to all the weird things going on around here. But I intend to get to the bottom of this, I can assure you."

"Right after you go upstairs and rest."

She nodded, her eyes drooping. "I am exhausted."

"I'll take you to your room."

"No need."

"I insist."

She marched ahead of Gabriel, but he caught up to her. "Malcolm is angry and he has a right to be. I knew not to take you out in the middle of the night. I'll give him a thorough update."

"Tell him I knew what I was getting into."

"Did you, Lara? Do you know how to handle killers and thugs, greedy, evil people who shoot first and never ask questions? Do you understand that art theft is considered a major crime by the FBI?"

She glared at him but hesitated as if carefully forming her words. "I don't need a lecture, Gabriel. I was there, remember?"

He stopped, stood back to take a breath. "And I should have kept you from being there. I could have gone alone to check on Herbert."

She whirled at the stairs. "No, I wanted to get out of the house…find some space…go on some sort of misguided adventure. But the reality of it is that a good man is dead and I don't know why. We were attacked and nearly killed last night. I'm glad we went out because now I can at least try to get to the bottom of this."

"With the proper procedure, which means letting the authorities investigate."

"I'll do that and more."

"And you'll cancel the event in the Quarter."

"No," she replied, turning to head upstairs. "If these people are bold enough to come at me the night of the gala, then they can do exactly that. I'll be ready for them, I can assure you."

Gabriel's heart twisted inside his chest. "You're much too bold and confident, Princess."

"I'm neither," she said, looking down at him. "But I refuse to be bullied anymore. We'll have people in place, and hopefully we can catch them in the act."

"Lara?" He touched a hand to her arm, wished he could hold her. "Don't be so brave."

"I don't have to be brave," she replied, her eyes sparkling a green-blue, her expression stubborn. "I have you for that."

Gabriel watched her walk up the stairs, her back straight, her pose regal. The woman had put a lot of trust in him. Now he had to live up to that trust. Did he dare admit to her that he'd failed before? Because one more stunt like last night's and he'd be out on his ear.

His phone buzzed again. With one last glance at Lara, he turned and went into the back of the house, hoping to find some privacy. The kitchen was empty.

"Murdock, you had one assignment. One lightweight, I-can-stay-out-of-trouble assignment. And what did you do?"

"I see you've heard the news."

Richard Littleton let out a colorful word. "The AP is all over this, Murdock. A European princess involved in a car chase in New Orleans and the driver just happened to be my best photojournalist—yeah, buddy, you can bet I'm interested. But not a peep from you. What's going on down there, anyway?"

Gabriel sank onto a barstool, longing for a strong cup of coffee. "It's complicated, Richard."

"Talk," his editor suggested.

So Gabriel told him the whole bizarre story. "The

press doesn't have the intimate details, but I do. I've got photos and copy, and I'm trying to get to the bottom of this. The Benoit is right there in the living room, magnificent and way too exposed. But this house is so full of security measures, it's tighter than an armored truck. I'm beginning to think whoever is harassing the princess isn't necessarily after the Benoit. More like they want her dead for some reason."

"Maybe she's seen or heard something that could ruin someone."

"I've been thinking the same thing," Gabriel admitted. "I'll get to the truth, one way or another. We've got a story here, Richard, and I intend to tell it with words and with pictures."

"You're in too deep to write a fluff piece now. I want the whole story. Art and crime equals ratings."

"Yes, I'm well aware of that," Gabriel said, too tired to get excited. "I'll get the real story."

"Are you sure you're up to this, Murdock? It's only been a few months."

"I don't have a choice," Gabriel retorted. "This time, though, I plan to keep the woman alive." He hung up and turned at the click of a heel.

And found Lara standing there staring at him in shock.

EIGHT

"Lara, do you want something to eat or drink?"

The princess had changed into a deep blue cotton lounge set, a long tunic over cropped leggings. The color brought out her eyes. Her angry, accusing eyes.

"I came down for a cup of tea, but I see I got here just in time. What is the real story, Gabriel?"

Gabriel braced his hands against the granite countertop. "It's not what you think."

"I believe it's exactly what I think. You've got your claws into a story about greed and murder and…thugs, maybe? A story that has scandal and power and meat, is that what you told your editor? Is that why you really came back to New Orleans?"

"Lara—"

She held up her hand and pushed past him to turn on the kettle. "Don't talk to me. Don't try to convince me. I've had so many letdowns this week, I can't take another."

"Lara?" He moved toward her, then stopped. He

wouldn't frighten her or put her in a corner. "My editor heard about our escapade last night. It's all over the newswires. I had to tell him the truth. There is another story here, and I intend to keep digging for the truth. But I won't release what I find unless you give me the word."

"How can I even begin to trust that?" she asked, her fingernails drumming against the granite near the gas burner. "This whole household is in an uproar, and I still don't know who's behind this. For all I know, you could be the one pulling the strings just to generate some attention."

"Yeah, sure. I put you through all of that last night just to get a better story. Surely you can't believe that?"

"I don't know what to believe," she said on a weary breath. The kettle started whistling so she grabbed it away and turned off the flame. "I couldn't sleep, so I thought maybe I'd have some tea and try to find some peace, but there is no peace here. Maybe there never was."

Gabriel's heart hurt for her. To the world, she was a spoiled, pampered princess. To him, she was a living, breathing soul who hurt and worried and wondered just like the rest of humanity. "Do you want me to ignore a major crime story?"

"We don't know if it's a major crime yet."

"Your compound has been breached twice and your chef is dead. Your assistant tried to run away, and we were almost killed a day ago and again last night. What more do you need to see the truth?"

"I do see the truth." She went about making her tea, then searched the walk-in pantry until she'd found some cookies.

Then she lifted up onto a barstool and stared into the steaming brew. "I do see the truth, more than anyone can know."

Gabriel did a slow approach and carefully slid in beside her. "Have you talked to Deidre this morning?"

"Briefly. She's upstairs in her room fielding calls from reporters. This is a story—you're right there. And it's going viral."

"All the more reason for me to tell the firsthand account so that the world will know the truth."

She turned to stare at him, a shortbread cookie in her hand. "And *you* want that firsthand *real* story, don't you?"

"I want to get pictures and write the text, yes. I want to make sure you're safe and that your work here won't be overshadowed by this scandal or these criminals."

She sat staring and silent.

Gabriel had a new thought. What if the princess did know more than she was willing to tell? Was that why she kept refusing to cancel any of her planned events?

He sat staring and silent beside her.

Finally, they both turned together and peered into each other's eyes.

"Gabriel, I—"

"Lara, can I—"

"You first," he said, his heart bracing while he took in her beautiful expression. He saw a flittering of regret, coupled with a second or two of trust.

She took a sip of her tea, broke her shortbread in half. "I wonder about this, all of it."

"And?"

"The Benoit has to be the reason for all of this. But then, that painting has been hanging in this house off and on for years. The security in this old place is top-notch but not impenetrable. If someone really wanted the painting, they could have easily broken in while I was away."

"And yet, they didn't." He nodded. "They waited for you to return."

"That makes me think they want something more."

Gabriel let out a sigh of relief. At least she was still willing to talk to him. And she was taking this seriously now. "Before we discuss this, are we good? I mean, do you understand I have my original assignment but now things have changed for me?"

"Things have changed for all of us." She bit into her cookie and chewed for a minute. "I don't like it, but I can certainly understand your need to know. I want to know, too."

He didn't dare move. "So do we work together, or do you want me to stick to the plan?"

"If I told you to cease and desist, would you?"

"Probably not," he admitted. "But I can promise you this. I won't do anything without your knowledge. Even if I catch these crooks red-handed, I won't print anything without you approving it. And that's a big concession for a photojournalist, for any journalist."

"Can you make that promise, even if you have to go against your magazine's wishes?"

He thought long and hard about that one. He'd never made concessions before. But this was Lara. "Yes," he finally said, knowing he might regret that later. But right now he couldn't leave this behind. He had a story to capture and he had a princess to protect.

But she needed to understand one more thing. "Lara, I was on assignment in the Middle East a few months back, and...I tried to help a woman there. I got involved in a squabble between her and her father. He didn't like the woman she'd become—strong, brave, independent. He tried to kill her."

"What happened?"

"I went off assignment and tried to get her out of the country. He found out and, true to his word, he had her killed before I could get back to take her away."

Lara's eyes went dark. "And you blame yourself?"

"Of course I do. I got in a world of trouble from the State Department and my boss, but I don't care. I had to help that woman. That's why I was re-assigned to come here with you." He shrugged, looked over at her. "This was supposed to be an easy assignment."

"Nothing about me is ever easy, Gabriel. I'm so sorry, but you can walk away at any time."

He shook his head. "That's my biggest flaw. I can't let go of a good story. And I certainly can't walk away from a woman in danger. So I'm afraid you're stuck with me."

She finished her tea and brushed the crumbs off her fingers. "I'm glad you told me the truth, but I'm sorry you blame yourself for what happened to your friend. Please don't blame yourself for anything that happens from here on out." Then she stood and smiled. "Would you like some breakfast?"

The princess made him toast with jam and cof-fee. They'd shared a few intimate moments there in the kitchen, mostly with him apologizing for taking her out last night and for talking to his editor about this before clearing things with her. Lara's formal-ity had softened with each apology, and he'd finally opened up to her about Adina. She poured him an-other cup of coffee and offered him more toast.

"Were you in love with her?"

"I cared about her. I only wanted to help her."

"It's not your fault, Gabriel. And last night is not your fault."

He wanted to believe her, but he somehow always wound up getting too involved. And he was way too involved with her.

They sat talking, sharing, gaining a new understanding.

Until Deidre breezed in and got all aghast at royalty serving a lowly photographer. She admonished Gabriel and grabbed Lara up and carted her up to her room to rest.

Deidre was a strange bird, no doubt. He intended to find out more about her. Maybe she'd been properly vetted, but Gabriel knew there were many ways to hide a person's true identity. He'd already sent Richard a list of names for thorough background checks. Starting with Malcolm Plankton and the team of men listed underneath him and ending with dear little Deidre Wilder.

So he'd sent Richard updates all day long and worked on editing his digital photos while Lara slept. She'd come back downstairs late in the afternoon, looking beautiful in spite of her obvious distress.

Then, while Deidre reassured anxious friends and supporters that the princess was safe, Lara and he had rearranged her schedule. Not even Deidre knew Lara's next move. She would tell the assistant at the last minute. This morning, Lara had canceled everything and asked to be left alone. Deidre had obliged and changed the appointment they'd had with the catering group coming to discuss food for the gala.

But the whole house was in mourning regarding Herbert's death. Gabriel and Lara had told the police the truth about that. They'd gone to check on him, and Gabriel had found him dead. Shot in the head, but he hadn't elaborated on that part.

Of course, Gabriel was probably high on the suspect list, but Lara had vouched for him. That meant she cared a little bit.

Cared. About him? Did he want her to care?

Yes. He did. Gabriel tried to deny that, but now, sitting here at a dainty desk in a quiet corner of the house, he had to admit he wanted Lara's respect. And maybe more. Much more.

Malcolm came clopping down the hallway. "A word with you, Mr. Murdock."

Gabriel stood, waited for the dour security guard to speak.

"Mrs. Kincade has requested that you move into the house during the duration of your assignment."

"And you disapprove, of course?" Gabriel could see the disdain on Malcolm's expanded jowls.

"I'm not pleased, but I'm not the boss. If the princess wants you here, then you're here." The stout, stoic man stepped close. "But if you pull another stunt like what happened last night, I'll personally knock you unconscious."

"Got it," Gabriel said, nodding. "I only want to keep Her Royal Highness safe, Malcolm."

"You can help all of us do that by staying out of things unless the princess or I give you permission to do otherwise."

Gabriel looked down at the floor. "What we did last night was dumb. Not one of my finest moments. It won't happen again."

"Then we both are agreed on that."

"She went back upstairs earlier. How is she?" Gabriel asked, knowing Malcolm had a guard at her door.

"I believe she's sleeping. Deidre is to wake her for a light supper."

"Good. She needs her rest."

"Yes." Malcolm peered at Gabriel as if he were a bug on the rug. "Now, if you'll excuse me."

"Of course." Gabriel sat back down. He stared at his laptop, thinking about how much he liked being around Lara. She was smart, pretty and adventurous. All traits he admired. But she was also thoughtful, caring and the real deal.

He'd definitely put that in the article.

The other article.

He'd let Adina down and it had cost her her life. He'd never know what might have been with the gentle, shy, dark-haired woman who only wanted to see America. But he did know he was not worthy of Adina giving her life.

He might not be worthy of this princess, either. But he could try to save *her* life.

Right now he wanted to go over the pictures he'd taken at the site of the crash. When he pulled up the file, he saw the shot he'd taken of the crowd of reporters outside the gate the other day. He enlarged the one of the man he'd noticed who seemed to stand out from the crowd. The stranger had not acted like a frantic reporter. No, he'd stood aside, his camera forgotten in his hand while he stared up at the house.

The same man who'd asked Lara so many pointed questions at the press conference. Who was he?

Gabriel worked the keys and zoomed in until the man's badge was enlarged enough that he could read the name on it.

Connor Randall. No affiliation to any local news stations, and Gabriel didn't recognize the logo on the lanyard. The emblem had the letters *MAI* in bright red with a white lightning streak running through the letters.

Gabriel did a search and came up with several organizations with that acronym. But only one that had the lightning strike tied to it. Louis Armond Industries. Something to do with energy and offshore drilling. Oil money. Headquartered in New Orleans, with locations and offices all over the world. When he searched the name Louis Armond, nothing much came up. Local businessman and entrepreneur, generous donor to all sorts of local causes. A force to be reckoned with in New Orleans.

Would Louis Armond be on Lara's VIP list for the upcoming gala?

Gabriel felt sure of it since the man was involved in so many local causes. So what was a man who was wearing a name tag from MAI doing standing in a group of reporters? Maybe he was a news junkie who'd wandered up to listen in with several of the interested neighbors.

Gabriel made a note in his pocket notebook, then turned back to the photos he'd downloaded. This time he went over the few he'd been able to capture with his cell phone at the site of last night's scene.

People were gathered around, staring down at the wrecked car. Gabriel zoomed in on one cluster of people.

And was shocked to find the same man standing out away from the crowd. Connor Randall again.

Interesting that the same mysterious man who had been at Lara's press conference and at her gate the day before had also been at the scene last night.

Why was Connor Randall hovering around? And how long had he been watching Lara?

Before Gabriel could form an opinion in his brain, Malcolm marched into the room. "It wasn't Herbert," he said, his frown etching his wizened face into a pucker. "Thank God for that."

"The dead man?" Gabriel stood, his own frown

matching Malcolm's. "If that wasn't Herbert, then who was it?"

"A friend who was staying at his apartment," Malcolm replied. "But this means Herbert Tullis is still missing. Let's all pray he's still alive."

Lara woke with a start.

The late-afternoon sun shimmered across the hardwood floors, its beams floating like a spotlight against the room's blue and white colors. A bit disoriented, she sat up and wiped at her eyes. How long had she slept?

The gilded clock on the bedside table told her it was almost seven at night. She lifted the covers and headed to the bathroom for a long shower.

She'd dreamed of Theo.

They'd been in the living room, talking about the Benoit.

"I bought it for you, darling. Only you."

"Why? I have everything I need."

"Not everything." He started walking away. "Not everything, my darling. It's a very special painting."

She cried out for him, but he was gone, and then she was lost in a mass of walls and paintings. She couldn't find her way out.

Lara asked God to help her understand, but she wondered if her prayers would bring her any peace.

After she'd had her shower and was dressed, she paged Deidre to come to her room so they could talk while she finished pulling herself together.

Deidre shuffled some papers, checked her tattered day calendar. "We need to approve the menu we picked. We only have a week."

"Then let's focus on that today," Lara said before dismissing Deidre.

Lara didn't tell Deidre that she'd agreed with Gabriel that rearranging things would give her an edge. If someone was planning these attacks based on her busy schedule then that someone would have to shuffle around to keep up with her now. It was a simple plan, but the first step in winning her life back.

And Gabriel would be with her, taking pictures and serving as an unofficial bodyguard. She did trust him with her life. She liked being around him, too. He was smart and worldly. He could move in any circle and hold his own. He treated her like a woman, not just a princess. She wasn't a princess anyway. That was just a title someone had tacked onto her. She was a woman and she was very much aware of him as a man. But his charm and her attraction went deeper than that. He knew people, knew how to take charge of things. That could either be annoying or something she could use as a blessing and an advantage. And after their heart-to-heart discussion this morning, Lara understood Gabriel's hesitation and his dedication.

He needed to be needed. He needed to redeem himself.

Dear Lord, how can I help this man? How can he help me?

You must only allow him to help you. You can't fall for this man. You have obligations, a reputation to uphold.

She thought about her dream again. Thought about Theo. Had her husband taken secrets to the grave with him?

Lord, You know my heart. I came here for answers and now I only have more questions. Help me to be still and wait, Lord.

Lara stared at herself in the vanity mirror, wondering how she'd get through all of her obligations without falling to pieces. Did someone think she knew her husband's secrets? Were these people willing to kill in order to get to those secrets? Or did they know she'd been secretly investigating her husband's death? The man she'd invited to the gala certainly should know. His actions were so obvious, he only confirmed Lara's suspicions. Now she had to prove her suspicions.

All the more reason to try to find the truth. With Gabriel Murdock's help. That meant she had to be careful, very careful, of losing her heart again. She also had to be careful of using a good man as a means to an end no one would see coming.

NINE

"You shouldn't venture out, madame."

Lara glanced from Malcolm's dour expression to Gabriel's puzzled one. "What do you think, Gabriel?"

She'd decided this morning that she *would* venture out, but no one in the house seemed to think that was a good idea. Lara wanted to shout that she knew her tormentor and he wouldn't dare try anything else, but she couldn't be sure. And she couldn't give up now.

Gabriel stood with feet planted apart. Was that his stance for arguing? This mixing things up had been his idea, after all.

"I appreciate that you want to continue with your plans, Your Highness. And I did suggest you rearrange your schedule."

Malcolm scowled at that.

She tapped her heel, impatient to get on with things. "But?"

Malcolm cleared his throat. "But there's something we didn't tell you last night."

Shocked, Lara glanced around. "What's happened now?"

Gabriel faced her. "Herbert is not dead. The body in his apartment—it wasn't him. Since you never actually saw the body, you couldn't have known. I assumed it was him. I was wrong."

"Oh, my." Lara put her hand to her pearls. "Oh, my. So Herbert is okay?"

"Still missing," Gabriel said. "The police told us the man we found was a friend of his."

"But how do the police know he's not Herbert?"

"From a picture they found of Herbert," Malcolm explained. "And from the DMV. His height and weight didn't match those of the victim."

Lara digested that information, her mind reeling with both relief and worry. "Where is Herbert, then?"

"We don't know," Malcolm replied. "But at least now we do have the attention of the New Orleans Police Department. They're actively searching for him."

Gabriel gave her a measured glance. "You could take a couple of days to do things around the house rather than exposing yourself to the public right now. Down in the Quarter, not so wise. The reporters would follow. Could cause a major dustup."

"I *have to* agree," Malcolm said, emphasizing the "have to" part.

Lara hated it when other people were right. But the uneasiness she felt at knowing someone had died in Herbert's apartment brought her back to reality.

"Oh, all right. I was just trying to be productive. But what can I do sitting around the house? Besides worry about Herbert, I mean?"

Gabriel shot Malcolm a calm smile. "I have an idea. I need to go over some background information with you and maybe get a few candid shots of you doing everyday things."

"Such as?"

"Phone calls, reading, signing off on a file. Normal things."

Lara let out a huff of breath. "Ah, I remember normal. And I miss it sorely. I did tell Deidre I'd go over the gala menu with her."

"All the more reason to stay here, safe and sound, and get that done," Malcolm said, the relief in his words palpable. "I have people looking for Herbert, so you don't have to go on that particular errand again."

Deidre, who'd been taking notes and scratching them out with each change of plans, smiled. "I could have the caterer send over some menu samples, ma'am. That way, you won't have to meet with the caterers here. If you approve the food today, we can mark that off the list."

"Good. I like marking things off the list. And we did get the invitations out, right?"

"Yes, ma'am. Earlier in the week," Deidre replied, her head down. "We're already receiving RSVPs." She ducked her head. "I think all the publicity has caused everyone to want to be a part of the gala."

"Isn't that great," Lara replied. "There will be articles suggesting I did all of this to make a stir."

"Don't read those articles," Gabriel suggested.

Lara saw the twinkle in his dark eyes. How did he manage to make her feel good even in such dire circumstances? "Thank you all for being so diligent." She'd included Gabriel in that, her gaze holding his.

"How many people are coming?" Gabriel asked.

"Maybe seventy-five," Deidre replied. "It's supposed to be an intimate night."

"And they'll pay a hefty price for that intimacy and the chance to bid on rare art pieces," Lara added. "That's how we raise money."

"And when do the other art pieces arrive?"

She gave Gabriel a surprised look. "The day before the event, for security purposes. We have them stored nearby, so that won't be a problem."

"Unless someone plans to make a hit on them in transport," Gabriel said.

"I'll have extra guards posted for the duration," Malcolm added. "Security will be extremely tight at both the warehouse and the gala. No one in or out without an invitation."

Gabriel rubbed his hands together. "So see, you

have more than enough to keep you busy here. We can go over that list, and you can tell us if anyone on the list might have some reason to harm you or to try and steal from you."

"These people have been longtime associates of my husband's," Lara retorted. "Surely you don't think any of them could be behind this?"

Malcolm cleared his throat again. "We always check for such things, Mr. Murdock."

"Of course you do," Gabriel replied. "But in this case, I'd say we need to double-check."

Malcolm gave him a reluctant nod. "I suppose that would be wise."

Lara saw the animosity between the two men. "Malcolm, I've given Gabriel full access to my everyday routine. Since he's been here from the beginning, I can't very well hide anything that happens from him. He's experienced in such matters, but don't think I've forgotten you are my head of security. You've done a good job so far, and I know I'll be safe with you in charge. Gabriel can add that little bit of extra security we need since he's familiar with New Orleans and he's been involved in such matters with other feature stories."

"It did all start once he arrived," Malcolm said, looking down his nose at Gabriel.

Deidre pushed at her glasses and stared at Gabriel.

Lara shook her head and ignored how she'd had the same doubts. She and Malcolm had both approved Gabriel. Her team knew the dangers they all faced, so why blame Gabriel? Besides, she was pretty sure about the man behind all of this. She just couldn't voice that assurance. "Enough of this. Gabriel is here to do a job, not sabotage us at every turn. I'll stay home today and take care of business over the phone. Understood?"

Everyone nodded. Malcolm shot Gabriel another suspicious glare. "I'll be nearby and watching, ma'am."

"I wouldn't have it any other way," Gabriel said.

"I agree." Lara turned to Deidre. "Would you print out a list of the people we're inviting to the gala, please? And bring me the mock-up for the menu. I'll mark which samples I'd like to test and you can order them."

"Certainly, ma'am."

Deidre and Malcolm both stomped off to do their jobs.

Gabriel turned to Lara with a twisted smile. "Whew."

She motioned to him, her pulse jumping at the realization that they had the whole day together. She should be used to having him by her side by now, but the man made her jumpy. "Let's go into my office."

"I can't blame them," he said behind her back.

She turned at her big antique desk. "Neither can I. There is a lot of distrust going around these days, I'm afraid."

He waited for her to sit; then he took a chair across from the desk. "Do *you* trust me?"

Lara put her hands together over her desk calendar. "I trust you as much as I trust anyone here, Gabriel. Don't make me regret that decision."

"I won't," he said. "But I do need to go over some things with you. I've been doing some research on my own."

This didn't surprise Lara. That was part of his job, part of what made him so good at that job. "And what have you found?"

"Do you know a man named Louis Armond?"

"Yes." She made a face. "He was a business associate of my husband's. I was forced to endure him at dinner parties and social events."

"Is he on the list for your upcoming event?"

She nodded. "I'd have to check, but I believe so. He's very generous within the art community."

"So he'd definitely be a donor for your cause?"

"He's likely to bid on several pieces of art during the auction in the Quarter."

"What else do you know about him?"

Lara's radar went up. "I told you—he's a local businessman. I don't know anything much beyond that. Why do you ask?"

"Someone wearing an ID with MAI on it was in the group of bystanders hanging out at your gate earlier this week."

"Louis Armond Industries. Why would an employee of his company be standing outside the gate with reporters?"

"My question exactly," Gabriel said. "The name on the ID was Connor Randall. Ever heard of him?"

Lara thought about that name. "No, not that I can recall."

Gabriel leaned up in his chair. "He's the bystander who hounded you at the press conference the other day. I have shots of him at the front gate here, and he was also on the scene after the crash last night."

She couldn't stop the gasp of shock. "Are you sure?"

"I have his picture, three times. He's either after a good story himself, or he's stalking you."

Lara didn't know what to say, but she didn't know the man he'd mentioned. "That is odd."

"And interesting. I think we should tell the police about this and let them investigate."

She nodded. "Of course. I wish I could remember more, but it's been so long since I've been here."

"He could just be a curious bystander or a big fan of royalty, but to find him at all three places is suspect. Especially him being at the crash site last night. For all we know, he could have been one of the men in the car."

She held back the shivers trying to skitter down her backbone. "I agree with that."

Deidre came into the room. "Here's the master list for the gala, ma'am. And the printout from the caterer."

"Thank you, Deidre. I'll get back to you with my menu choices."

Deidre shot a covert glance at Gabriel. "Would you like me to set up the sunroom for a photo session, Mr. Murdock?"

Gabriel took his time sweeping his gaze over Lara. By the time he'd finished appraising her, she felt as if he'd stared into her soul. "I think that might work. Thank you."

Deidre left as quickly as she'd appeared. Lara worried about her high-strung assistant. She still wanted to ask Deidre about her real reason for trying to run away the other day. Feeling the need to defend her, however, Lara said, "She likes to stay busy."

"Good thing," Gabriel replied. "So, we can go over the list now, and I'll set up for the shoot later this afternoon when the light in the sunroom is better."

Lara dreaded that. "Should I change?"

He smiled. "I like that dress. We'll try a few with it, if you don't mind."

"No, not at all." Had she picked the light baby-blue full-skirted dress to please herself...or Gabriel? Well, it was one of her favorite couture designs. And she'd wear it whenever it pleased her. But she couldn't help but blush a bit at his compliment. "And the pearls?"

"Leave the pearls, too," he said, his gaze lingering on her neck.

Feeling the heat of a blush creeping over her skin, she nodded. "All right, then. I'll order some coffee and water, and we'll go over the list."

His self-assured smile stayed with her until the coffee arrived. When she suggested they move to the settee by the fireplace, he readily agreed.

And too late, Lara realized this settee wasn't really made for two people. Gabriel was so close she could see his thick dark eyelashes and the flecks of gold in his lion eyes.

She thought she also saw something else there, too.

The same awareness she felt in her heart.

Lara tried to hold her coffee cup steady, but having Gabriel so near was her undoing. The man made this femininely decorated office shrink to the size of a dollhouse. He filled it with a definite masculinity that had been missing from this house for a long, long time.

And from her life.

But was she ready to turn from being a widow to finding a new companion or a new love? Was she ready to move on from the deep, abiding love she still felt for her husband to dally with a man she'd only just met a few days ago? No, not until she'd done what she'd come here to do. That had to be her focus right now.

"What's wrong?"

She glanced up to find Gabriel peering at her with a concerned frown. "Oh, nothing. Just thinking. I miss Theo."

The concern on his face turned to compassion. And regret. "Of course you do. I'm sure you're used to having him at these big, fancy events."

"We did everything together," she said. Her hand shook as she tried to put her cup and saucer on the table.

Gabriel held her hand steady, then took the coffee cup from her. "Let me."

Lara pushed at a loose curl and tucked it behind her ear. "I think I'm having a delayed reaction to everything that's happened this week."

He took her hand back in his, gave her a gentle pat. "We can do this later."

Why did his touch make her feel all warm and fuzzy, silly, like a schoolgirl? "I... No...I'm fine. I need to stay busy."

"Okay. If you're sure."

"Of course." She pulled her hand away and sat up straight. "Back to the list." She grabbed it like a lifeline and pretended to read the names there. When she saw the name Louis Armond, she pointed, relieved to find something substantial to concentrate on. "He's on the list, Gabriel. Mr. Armond."

Gabriel's attention changed from her to the list with immediate clarity. "Okay, it's a start. Would he have any reason to come after you?"

"Not that I know of," she said, trying to remember. "Theo had a lot of associates, but I didn't always know them. We'd see them briefly on social occasions when we were here, but for the most part, Theo took care of the business details while I worked with our philanthropic endeavors."

"So you never had any type of long-standing contact with Mr. Armond?"

"No." She hesitated, then said, "But the man did make me feel strange. He's a big flirt. The kind that makes inappropriate remarks and stares at women a little too keenly."

"I know the kind," he replied, his gaze sweeping over her face. "If he makes you uncomfortable, there has to be something there."

"So you think my intuition is sending me a warning?"

"Could be. We can't accuse him without reason, though, even if he is a flirt. Now that we know he's invited, we can certainly pay special attention to him the night of the gala."

"That should be interesting. He usually has a lovely young lady on each arm."

"We'll watch them, too. You never know about people."

"No, you don't." She stared down at the list to hide the deception in her eyes. "I do remember Theo feeling much the same way I do about him. A necessary business partner, but not someone Theo was that chummy with." As far as she knew. She glanced around to make sure they were alone. "This is strictly unsubstantiated gossip, but the rumor in New Orleans social circles is that Mr. Armond is part of a long-standing Mafia group."

Gabriel's eyes flashed a deep gold. "Are you sure about that? I don't know the man, but I've been out of the city for a lot of years now."

"No. As I said, it's gossip."

"Most gossip begins in truth," he said, his gaze solemn. "And if that is true, we have a bigger problem than we thought. That would mean he's a very dangerous, ruthless man."

"And we almost pushed two of his henchmen into the river last night."

"Yes, we did try, but they managed to get away." Gabriel jotted a few notes in his pocket notepad. "I need to check this out a little more. I might need to go downtown, talk to some people in the know."

Lara's heart raced ahead of her thoughts. What if she'd pegged the wrong man? "Do you think he could be the one behind all of this?"

"If he's an art lover and he wants the Benoit, he might be trying to scare you away. But as you said, he could have easily stolen it while the house was empty."

Lara knew now was the time to come clean regarding the Benoit. "I have a confession to make, Gabriel."

"I'm listening."

"The Benoit in the living room is the real one, but when I'm away—"

"You put a fake one in its place?"

"Yes. I don't like admitting that and very few people know it, but Theo used to insist—for insurance purposes and because he never wanted to lose the original. It's always put in storage in a climate-controlled warehouse when we're not in residence."

"Is this the same warehouse where the rest of the auction items are being held?"

"Yes."

Gabriel got up to pace around. "That brings up a new concern. What if Armond knows you do the switch and he wants the real one anyway?"

"But how could he know?"

"If he's the man you described, he'd have a way to know anything he wants to know."

Lara put a hand to her throat. "Such as questioning people around me? Like Herbert?"

"Yes. Or maybe he tried to enlist Herbert's help and when Herbert refused…" Gabriel came to sit back down. "We have to consider every possibility. He could have hired the mysterious Connor Randall to do his dirty work. This scenario is beginning to make a lot of sense."

A new fear poured through Lara, causing her heart rate to rise. What if she'd been wrong all along? "He wouldn't dare try anything at the gala, would he?"

"We can't predict that," Gabriel said, "but we can be prepared."

"I intend to be just that," Lara replied. "But first,

find out anything you can about the man. I don't want to accuse him without strong evidence to back it."

"I'm on it," Gabriel replied. "Let's finish going over the list, and I'll do a little research and go by the police station before we do the photo session later today."

"All right." Lara hated the scenarios of danger running through her head, but knowing they might be onto something sent a buzz of hope through her system. If she could figure out who was behind all these attacks, then she could move on with her own plans. But then, she had decided the person she needed to talk to and the person behind all this activity had to be one and the same.

When she looked up and saw Gabriel's confident smile, she came close to telling him what she'd held in her heart for so long. But...no. This was something she had to do on her own.

TEN

Gabriel left the New Orleans police station armed with information regarding Louis Armond. While the detectives he'd interviewed held most of what they knew close to their vests, so to speak, he'd gotten enough out of them to realize Armond was a very rich, very dangerous man.

"He goes after what he wants, and he goes after anyone who stands in his way," one of the detectives had said. "We'll keep him on the radar regarding Princess Lara Kincade."

Gabriel wondered at that. They hadn't gotten anywhere with finding the missing chef, and they couldn't verify the identity of the friend lying in the city morgue, nor were they willing to discuss Connor Randall.

"Probably another curiosity-seeker," one detective had said. "But we'll run a check on him and get back to you."

They'd been rather tight-lipped on the whole investigation. Maybe they realized they'd dropped the ball on investigating Herbert, so now they didn't want to give up any inside information. Or maybe someone was pulling their strings.

Gabriel would have to make a note of that and conduct his own background search regarding the chef. In the meantime, he did manage to get a picture of the Benoit-like print someone had left on the upstairs balcony. Maybe he could compare that one with the real Benoit hanging in Lara's house and find something that gave them a hint.

His cell rang while he was walking across Jackson Square.

"Murdock, what kind of mess have you stumbled across?" asked Richard.

"I don't know, but I'm beginning to think this story has deep roots. Do you have something for me?"

Richard coughed and cleared his throat. "The Wilder girl is clean. Good grades, college grad, the works. I'm pretty sure she ran her own lemonade stand when she was a kid."

"I can see her doing just that," Gabriel replied, smiling. "I don't know why she gives me the creeps, but she does. And she did try to run away, but she's back now and seems to be calm. As calm as a type A can be, I suppose. Anything else?"

"Malcolm Plankton—interesting. He used to be a butler, but two years before Prince Theo died, he promoted Malcolm to head of security. Malcolm has credentials. He served in the army and went to officer training school at a Royal Military Academy. How he went from that to being a butler is beyond me, but he was one for ten years before the prince put him in security. Seems to have a spotless record."

"Maybe he was more than a butler all those years. Military men make great adjutants even after they leave the military."

"Could be. As I said, he's well educated and capable."

"Okay. What about the list of guards?"

"Clean as choirboys. Not a rap sheet amongst them."

"So it might not be anyone on the staff," Gabriel replied, his gaze scanning the Square. "I'll have to keep an eye on the underlings and see if anyone acts suspicious."

"The chef has a checkered past, all tablecloths aside."

Gabriel shook his head at Richard's dry humor. "And?"

"He's been in and out of trouble. Owes some gambling debts."

"Interesting. I wonder if he knows Louis Armond."

"From what we've both discovered, Armond keeps tabs on those who owe him. Maybe he hired the chef away from the princess."

"Yeah, with a deal Herbert couldn't refuse. Thanks, Richard."

"Anything else you need?" Richard asked. He barked orders to several people in passing.

"I'm liking the chef," Gabriel said, used to Richard shouting out orders even while he talked on the phone. "He's still AWOL, but the police seem a little lackadaisical on getting the word out. Armond may be pulling those strings. And the two men who chased us have also disappeared. But this Connor Randall has to be involved. He's been on the scene a lot, but no one's saying why. Not even the locals."

"I'll keep my ear to the ground," Richard said. "Got to go."

And that was the end of that conversation.

Gabriel glanced around. The crowd milling around the Square was sparse, but it was the middle of the week. He spotted the usual street artists and musicians, the tarot-card readers and the trinket trolleys. Samuel the saxophone player was in his usual spot in front of the Café Du Monde. About as normal as a New Orleans afternoon could be.

Lara had told him the gala and art auction would take place in an old mansion right off the Square. Each room would be set up for a silent auction open to the public, and the live auction would take place upstairs in what used to be a small ballroom. The whole event was a private affair, but that didn't mean someone off the street couldn't find a way in.

He headed for the address she'd given him. It wouldn't hurt to check out the venue and get some preliminary shots for the magazine. When he saw a sign for Le Manoir du Jardin he knew he'd found the right place. The mansion fit right in with the other eclectic buildings just off the Square. It was white, two-storied and had intricate wrought-iron balconies surrounding both floors. Gabriel went to the door that had a sign that said Office over it.

"Hello there," a young, dark-haired woman said from behind a mahogany desk. "Can I help you?"

Gabriel smiled and flashed his credentials. "I'm here to do some scouting for possible photography areas for Princess Lara Kincade's event, scheduled here next week."

The girl looked doubtful. "Yes, we're all excited about that. Should I call her to confirm?"

"You may," Gabriel said. He gave her Deidre's cell number. "Her assistant can vouch for me."

The girl dialed and waited, giving him a quick smile even if she didn't look convinced. After reporting the information, she nodded. "Thank you so much. We just wanted to make sure."

She placed the phone back in its cradle. "Can't be too careful when it comes to a princess. We've been keeping up with the news about the recent harassment she's had to endure. We've already had a security team do a thorough sweep."

"Really?" Gabriel found that odd since the event was more than a week away. Malcolm hadn't mentioned doing a preliminary sweep. "When was that?"

"Earlier today. Two men. They just left." The

girl glanced out at the street. "They had credentials, too."

Gabriel got that burning in his gut. "I see. Well, that's not my concern. I'll only be a few minutes."

The girl smiled and pointed. "Take your time. We have one big dinner tonight, so the ballroom is already set up for that. Look but don't touch."

Gabriel held up his camera. "And I can snap some shots?"

"Of course. We don't allow patrons to bring in cameras, so you'll have to be the official photographer for the event. We have to preserve the antiques. You know, old rugs and curtains, such stuff as that."

"I understand. I'll be very careful."

He took the carpeted stairs. Impressed with the rich walnut banisters and the intricate curve of the free-floating stairway, he made his way to a remarkable stained-glass full-length window. A surveillance camera blinked discreetly off to the side of the window. That was good. Probably had those all over the house since it was full of antiques and art. Gabriel got a quick shot of the window. It would be a good backdrop for some shots of the princess with a few of her major donors.

Next, he turned right toward what he figured was the ballroom. It was done in dark paneling and showcased a marble fireplace and red velvet drapery. The big, paned windows looked out onto a beautiful square garden complete with a big, open courtyard. The long, polished table was set with glistening white china, sterling-silver dinnerware and sparkling crystal goblets.

Who knew such a place could be hidden away here in the Quarter. No wonder Lara liked this spot. It was a good venue for a big party and kept everyone away from her Garden District home.

But it was also the kind of place that gave security teams massive headaches. This old house had passageways to nowhere and cubbyholes everywhere. The ballroom had only one main exit inside the house, but it did have French doors that opened out onto the balconies on both the front and back of the house.

Gabriel went across the aged hardwood floor and opened a door that showed narrow stairs. The servants' entrance. He also spotted a dumbwaiter that probably still served as a means to get food up to the ballroom. It was big enough that a person could easily squeeze inside.

He got a few more shots in the ballroom. Then, after checking a powder room and two locked doors he assumed were bedrooms or storage areas, he decided to go down to the courtyard and get some photos of the garden. He took one more look at the ballroom, noting exit doors and a double-back staircase that curved on both sides off the long balcony that led to the gardens below.

He was headed back downstairs when a movement caught his eye out in the garden.

A dark-haired man was hurrying away from the

house, heading for a white gate at the back of the walled property. The man turned once and stared up at the ballroom.

It was the same man Gabriel had seen several times before.

Connor Randall.

Lara took another bite of the cream puffs. "Nice," she said, smiling over at Deidre. "I think we'll go with that one for dessert. I love éclairs."

"Me, too," Deidre replied, clearly enjoying this late lunch of sample foods.

"Now the finger sandwiches." Since Lara had taken her antidepressant before coming downstairs, she needed to eat anyway. She picked up a dainty little square. "What's this one?"

"Cream cheese and nuts with pepper jelly," Deidre replied. "It's rather tasty."

Lara bit into the sandwich and sat back to enjoy the sensation of the nuts mixed with the spicy jelly. "I like that. A lot."

They moved on to several more appetizers, some made with puff pastry and shrimp and some in the form of meat pies, a dish made famous in Louisiana. Following that, they enjoyed tender roast-beef sliders—something the caterer had suggested as modern and fun. Marinated crab claws came next.

"Mmm, the crab claws are wonderful. But the Dijon mustard on these sliders has some very strong horseradish in it," Lara said after nibbling one of the round little sandwiches. "Quite strong, but I do like it. And we'll have fresh shrimp and rémoulade sauce, as requested." She turned back to the dessert tray. "The petits fours are wonderful. Let's go with those and the cream-puff éclairs. Oh, and those yummy red-velvet mini-cupcakes, too."

After several rounds of samples, Lara stood up. "I think I've had enough." She marked the samples she liked and made a face at the ones she didn't want. "Will you fax our final choices back to the caterer, Deidre?" She stopped, put a hand to her pearls. "I miss Herbert. He was going to help with this. Remember, he wanted to make a special cake for the gala."

Deidre nodded, tears forming in her eyes. "I liked Herbert, a lot. I'll sure miss him. I hope he comes home soon."

Lara's eyes misted over. "It's horrible, the thought that we found another person dead. I pray Herbert is all right." No matter where he was, Herbert would want her to do what she'd set out to do. "I'm not in the mood for any of this, but I can't back out now. That would mean these evil people will win out. We can't let that happen."

Deidre lowered her head, her eyes downcast. "No, ma'am. I'm so sorry I tried to run away. I was just so scared. I still am, but I won't abandon you again."

"I'm fearful, too," Lara replied. "I've had a couple of phone calls. Our special guest has RSVP'd to

me personally, but do not put his name on the list."
She moved around the desk and put her hands on
Deidre's arms. "You did nothing wrong, so don't
feel guilty. I do appreciate your loyalty."

Deidre stared at her sensible brown pumps. "I
didn't think about Herbert or you or anyone else. I
only wanted to get away."

Lara wondered again if the girl had told her everything. Maybe everyone in this house had their
own secrets. "Deidre, if you ever need to talk—
about anything, you know you can come to me,
right?"

"Yes, ma'am. I'll be okay. It's just my half brother
got into some trouble a few years ago, and he ended
up going to prison. Having the police around has
brought all of that back."

Lara hid her shock. "I'm so sorry. I never knew
that. I remember you had a half brother, but I
thought he was living in New York."

"He did live there, but he returned to Europe for
a little while. He got caught up in some sort of conspiracy and got in over his head. He didn't do the
things they said, but he was sent to prison anyway."

"Is there anything I can do to help?"

"No, ma'am." Deidre stared off into space. "He's
out of jail now. I...I hope he doesn't try to track
me down."

"Is that what you're worried about?"

"A little," Deidre replied. "I don't want him
bringing trouble to your door."

Lara's nerves did a jump. "Could it be him? The one who's harassing us?"

"I hope not," Deidre replied.

"I appreciate your honesty." Lara's hand started shaking. She wished she could be truthful with everyone. "Goodness, I think I'm more exhausted than I realized."

"You should rest, ma'am."

"Yes. I think you're right." Lara blinked, dizziness overcoming her, white-hot heat rushing through her body, her nerves itching with fire. "I'll go lie down awhile before Gabriel sets up the next photo session."

Deidre waited while Lara walked toward the stairs. "Are you sure you're all right?"

Lara grabbed the polished wood railing. "Yes. I took a pill earlier, and they always make me sleepy. I've lost so much sleep, I think I could nap the rest of the afternoon. But wake me in about an hour." Gabriel was supposed to take some pictures of her later, but she wasn't sure she could keep awake during the sitting.

"If Mr. Murdock returns before I wake, would you ask him if we could postpone the photo shoot until tomorrow—after I've had a good night's sleep?"

"Yes, ma'am."

Lara made it to her bedroom on the other side of the hallway. Not bothering to take off her dress, she kicked off her pumps and fell across the big bed.

Before she knew it, her head was spinning and she felt faint again.

Maybe I'm just sleepy, she told herself before her world went black.

Gabriel was ten feet behind Connor Randall. He'd followed the man all the way around the Square, and now he planned to approach Mr. Connor and ask him outright what he was doing.

But his cell rang. Yanking it out of his pocket, he saw Deidre's number.

"Hello?"

"Mr. Murdock, you have to come back to the house right away!"

Gabriel's gaze followed Connor Randall as the other man crossed the street, headed toward the Moon Walk. "Why? What's wrong?"

"It's Princess Lara. She's taken ill. I've called 911, but I'm worried. She doesn't look so good. And she seems to be confused. She's asking for Prince Theo."

"I'm on my way."

He put away his phone. Then, after taking one last look at the man vanishing into the crowd, Gabriel started running toward the nearest taxi.

ELEVEN

Lara tried to get up out of the bed but her feet felt like mush and her legs wobbled. Her moist skin hissed a sweat-drenched fire. At the sound of footsteps, she grabbed at the teakwood bedpost and lifted up, but her vision blurred into a misty cloud. She saw a man standing in the door. Then she blinked and saw two, maybe three of him. He entered the room and whispered in her ear.

"Don't forget to take your medicine, Lara."

She heard his hand scraping across the nightstand. "I left two pills for you right here." Then he helped her back into bed.

She needed to tell him she'd already taken a sedative. She tried to speak, but a dark fog of fatigue tugged her back into blackness. The shadow moved across the dark room and disappeared. Lara gave in to the need to go to sleep.

"Lara?"

Who was calling to her? Why did he seem so far away?

"Lara?"

"I…" She reached out, trying to grab on to something. Still groggy, she tried to stand.

The man moved toward her, calling her name. Gabriel?

Lara tried to hold out her hand, twisted, her head spinning. She didn't want to give in to the heat, to the darkness. Her entire body seemed to be on fire.

"I can't—"

She couldn't speak even though her mind was screaming. She tried to lift up. Gabriel rushed toward her, taking her by her shoulders. When she sensed his hands on her, she fell into his arms, her head spinning when he held her. She stared up into his eyes, trying to tell him that something wasn't right.

But before she could get out the warning, her world shifted and a deep blackness hovered over her until she finally closed her eyes and gave in to the need to sleep.

"Lara? Lara, listen. Help is on the way. The ambulance is here. Do you hear me?"

Lara tried to speak, but the darkness kept dragging her down. Her insides itched with a racing fire that felt like tiny needles stabbing at her from every direction.

"Gabriel?" Had she called out or was she just imagining this? Was Gabriel even here? She tried to open her eyes. When she looked through the mist of pain, she thought her husband was standing there.

"Theo? Theo."

A woman's voice echoed over her fear and shock. "Rest, ma'am. The paramedics are here."

Deidre? What was going on? Was Theo alive?

Her heart burst with joy only to be replaced with despair. "You can't be here. You're dead. Theo, talk to me, please."

"It's me." A masculine voice. Theo? "It's me, Gabriel."

"Theo? I want Theo."

The man stepped away. "The paramedics are here now, Lara. You'll be all right."

She blacked out again before she could call his name. But in her mind she was screaming. She wouldn't be all right. She needed him. Him.

"Gabriel?"

But he'd already left the room.

Gabriel sat down in the parlor, his hands on the arms of the comfortable, high-backed chair. He wasn't much of a praying man, but he'd sent up a few requests to God to help Lara.

She'd been hallucinating. She'd called him Theo, or at least she thought she'd seen Theo. Why did that make him so fidgety and on edge?

The princess still loved her husband.

Of course she did. The woman had fallen in love, and it was only natural she'd still mourn the husband she'd adored. And how had he died? Oh, yes, a hunting accident?

To distract himself, Gabriel pulled out his phone and did a search of Prince Theodore Kincade. The results netted several long, drawn-out titles and over a dozen long, in-depth articles.

The prince had once been considered a playboy. Some of the circles he'd been a part of weren't exactly prince material. When Gabriel found a newspaper photo of the young prince at a party in Paris with none other than Louis Armond, Gabriel's intuition went on high alert. The picture had been taken ten years earlier, but...

There was also a long article about the hunting accident that had killed Prince Theodore. After talking to several eye witnesses, including the two bodyguards who'd been with the prince at the remote hunting lodge somewhere up above New Orleans, the authorities had ruled the shooting as a terrible accident. The prince had been walking through the woods near the lodge and another hunter had seen movement. He thought he saw a deer, so he took aim. And accidentally shot the prince, who was wearing camouflage. While conspiracy theories filled the airwaves and the internet, the authorities had conducted a long investigation and declared it an accident.

Gabriel finished the article and saw the picture of Lara standing alone by her husband's casket. What an awful time that must have been. No wonder she still called out to her husband. She needed answers, too.

Interesting. Did Lara know her husband had been close to Armond? She'd mentioned they'd invited him to social events but that he made her feel uncomfortable. Maybe the prince liked having the powerful businessman around. Now Gabriel wondered about the "accident" at the hunting lodge. Had Louis Armond been on that trip? The article talked about a man named Frederick Cordello as the one who'd accidentally pulled the trigger. There wasn't much more information on him. He'd apparently gone into hiding, fearing for his life.

Gabriel made a note of several of the other names associated with the young prince, but Armond was the only name that stood out—other than Cordello. What was his story?

Then he pulled up a picture of the wedding.

Lara, in a demure white, flowing gown, a long veil cascading over her upswept hair.

The woman was beautiful.

Please, God. Take care of her for me.

He closed the page so he wouldn't sit there and stare at a woman he had no business thinking about in terms other than business. He needed to get his work done and get out of New Orleans. He was treading through dangerous territory. On very familiar territory. Thoughts of Adina's dark, laughing eyes haunted him, making him think he was too vulnerable when it came to beautiful women.

Gabriel had never been the settling-down kind, but sitting here now thinking about Lara made him wonder if it wasn't time to do just that. It was probably just the adrenaline rush of hitting on a mystery that could turn into a great page spread. While that was exciting, this puzzle was also dangerous. Very dangerous. He needed to focus on this developing story. He needed to remember that Lara Kincade was still in love with her husband and that she was not interested in a man she hardly knew. A man who traveled a lot and roamed the earth searching for that perfect shot that would tell a story. He'd come close to something else with Adina, but he'd resisted it so he could save her. But he'd failed. The story made headlines, but Gabriel's grief had been pushed aside.

And now he had to do the same. Push everything aside to get to the truth.

He went over the threats yet again.

A voodoo doll.

An intruder who'd left a miniature rendering of what looked like a Benoit, but one few people had ever seen.

A near-fatal crash from a punctured tire.

An unidentified dead man and a missing chef.

And now a very ill princess. Food poisoning or deliberate poisoning? Maybe something else, even worse.

He had to find the people who were harassing Lara. He also had to find out why they were after her. Glancing up at the Benoit, he got up to stare at the painting. Was there something there? A hint of things to come?

He studied the painting, dividing it into squares so he could use the rule of thirds. In his mind, he slashed the painting with two horizontal and two vertical lines so he could pinpoint the main focus of the painting.

His eyes landed on a woman holding a basket. Gabriel studied the basket and realized it had some sort of emblem on it. The fleur-de-lis-shaped design held several swirls and the word *UN*. United, maybe? A word or initials? *Un*. That meant *one* in French. Intricate artwork? Or a symbol? He jotted down his thoughts so he could research the painting later.

He studied the emblem once again, wondering where he'd seen something like that before. Maybe he was remembering it from the first time he'd walked into this room and seen the painting.

Or maybe he'd seen it somewhere else in New Orleans.

Before he could gather his thoughts, Deidre came running downstairs. "She's going to be all right, Mr. Murdock." She rushed toward Gabriel, then turned and glanced around, a frightened look on her face.

"What is it?" Gabriel asked, learning to read the girl's distress.

Her whisper floated to the rafters. "The paramedics think she had a bad reaction to something she ate."

"Food poisoning?" Gabriel remembered Lara going over the sample menu for the gala. "Did you both test the food for the event coming up next week?"

Deidre bobbed her head. "We did. We each tasted the same appetizers."

"But you feel okay?"

Deidre pushed her glasses up on her nose. "Yes, I do. I don't understand. Maybe what she had for breakfast."

"She had a couple of cookies. Just like yesterday."

"She loves homemade oatmeal cookies with her tea," Deidre replied. With a sad expression, she whispered, "Herbert always made them for her. I'll check the pantry and see what we have."

"I think she had a couple of tea biscuits or maybe shortbread." Gabriel wished he'd been more attentive this morning to the food instead of the woman. "She was exhausted and upset that Herbert was still missing, so she didn't eat very much. She did slice a banana and shared that with me."

Deidre stepped forward. "Mr. Murdock, you don't think I had anything to do with this, do you?"

Gabriel wasn't quite sure how to answer that question. Deidre had suggested ordering the samples. So he did the opposite. "Did you?"

Deidre's eyes misted over. "No, sir. Of course

not. I told Her Royal Highness why I almost left the other day."

"Can you tell me?"

Deidre nodded. "It's my half brother. He got into some trouble a while back—while he was in Europe. He was in jail over there, but I've heard since that he received a pardon thanks to a stranger's kindness."

Gabriel wondered about the girl's ramblings. "I'm sorry about your brother, Deidre. But what does that have to do with your leaving the other day?"

She twisted her dark hair. "I was afraid the police would associate me with that and…think I was up to no good."

"But you weren't, of course."

"No. Just scared and homesick. I was afraid he might be in New Orleans stirring up trouble. I won't abandon Princess Lara. She needs me."

That was an interesting way to put it. Gabriel didn't pursue questioning the girl, but the half-brother factor was intriguing. "Is the princess resting now?"

"Yes, but she wanted me to come and tell you that she's fine now. They gave her some antinausea medicine and something to counter the reaction."

"Reaction? I thought it was food poisoning."

"They don't know for sure."

When they heard voices, Gabriel and Deidre both looked toward the foyer. The paramedics were leaving.

"Hold up," Gabriel called, wanting to get the diagnosis from the source. "How is Princess Lara?"

Both men looked jaded and tired. The taller one said, "She's resting. We gave her an antidote to curb the reaction to the mushrooms."

Gabriel turned to Deidre. "She ate mushrooms?"

"Not that I know of," Deidre replied, a hand to her throat. "She's highly allergic, so we never order food with mushrooms."

One of the paramedics pivoted around. "She kept mentioning that she was allergic to mushrooms, that she'd had this kind of reaction before."

"And codeine," the other one said. "She refused any medicine that had codeine."

"Deidre, did you know she was allergic?"

"Yes, but we didn't eat anything with mushrooms in it."

The EMTs glanced at each other, then back to Gabriel. "Hey, man, the lady upstairs said she's highly allergic to mushrooms, so we think that's what she ingested. If she gets worse, she'll need to go to the emergency room. She refused transport."

"And that's all you're allowed to say," Gabriel replied. "I know the privacy laws. Thank you."

Malcolm showed up to escort the men out, leaving Gabriel alone with Deidre. "I'm not accusing you," he said, his tone low and non-threatening. "If the caterer knew not to send anything with mushrooms in it then I suggest you'd better call and check on that. They might have been working with mushrooms and somehow got some into the food they prepared for your tasting. Allergies can be so serious they sometimes cause death, you know."

"I understand that," Deidre retorted, anger coursing through her words. "I told the caterer that, too."

"Who's the caterer, then?"

Deidre let out a breath and regained her composure. She named the place. "Would you like the number so you can verify?"

Gabriel shook his head. "No. I know it's not my place to boss you around, but I'm concerned. I've only been here a few days and none of them have been pleasant. I'm supposed to be doing a positive, encouraging photo session with the princess. But I find I'm caught in the middle of some sort of harassment case." He walked toward Deidre, who stood by a desk. "I intend to find out who's behind all of this, so I can do my job. But mostly, so your princess will still be alive by the time I leave here."

Deidre bobbed her head again. "I understand. I'll call the caterer right now." She turned to leave. "Oh, and she wanted to see you. When she wakes up. She was falling asleep when I left her earlier."

"I'll be right here," Gabriel replied, sorry that he'd been so brusque with the girl earlier. "Thank you, Deidre." He sank down by the desk. "And, Deidre, we'll get this figured out. You don't have to run every time you see a policeman. Or me, for that matter."

"Thank you." The girl lifted her chin and scurried out of the room.

Leaving Gabriel to stare up at the fascinating painting that seemed to be the key to all of this.

What did it all mean?

Gabriel loved solving puzzles. Probably part of the reason he'd become a photojournalist. He liked to take a picture and then figure out the real story behind it. The old cliché was so true—a picture really did tell a thousand words.

The Benoit was a portrait within a portrait—a rendering of the Arcadian people who'd been run out of their Canadian homes of Nova Scotia, Quebec and other areas of Canada in 1755. But it was also a pastoral full of harmony and an unspoiled wilderness that made the portrait look almost like a dream or a vision.

He looked again and saw a shepherd out in a field, watching over the people below who seemed to be gathering food. Gabriel stared at the big woven basket again. UN. One?

Could that be a code for the first of the supposedly three Benoits? Did the three tell a tale that someone wanted to bring to light? Or to keep hidden?

He remembered the tiny painting Lara had found on the upstairs balcony. Who had painted that? And did they just guess at it? The police had that painting and the voodoo doll. Had he seen something there? Remembering the quick photo he'd snapped of the voodoo doll and the copy of the Benoit print the police let him see, Gabriel decided he needed to see that rendering and the voodoo doll with his own eyes. If the smaller fake had a fleur-de-lis with the word *DEUX* on it, he might be onto something. But did that mean the intruder had the other painting or that he thought Lara had it?

The voodoo doll could mean something else entirely.

Either way, he had a lot of digging to do before nightfall.

He wanted to find out about mushrooms and he needed to go through his photo files.

He was on his way out the door when his cell rang.

"Gabriel?"

Lara? She sounded raspy and tired. "Lara, are you all right?"

"Could you come up to my suite, please?"

"Of course." He hurried up the stairs, his thoughts swirling like the dream clouds in the Benoit.

TWELVE

Lara listened for Gabriel. When she heard a soft knock, she tried to raise her head. "Come in." She fell back down on the pillow, her head spinning again. Groggy and disoriented, she watched as he crossed the room.

"How are you feeling?" Gabriel asked, standing near the side of the bed. "Shouldn't you have a nurse?"

"I'm okay." She pointed to her cell phone and a walkie-talkie on the nightstand. "I have all the modern modes of communication nearby."

"Good." He took a quick glance around the room.

Lara wondered what he must think about this fancy, expensively decked sanctuary. "Are you uncomfortable?" she asked.

"Me, no." He looked confused. Maybe he was just avoiding her. "I…uh… Did you need something?"

She nodded, swallowing her fears. "I think someone deliberately put mushrooms in some of that food."

"Yes, I agree on that. You specifically told Deidre no mushrooms. Did the EMTs determine that?"

"No. They said I'd have to go to a hospital to be tested. I can't do that. The press would swarm the place."

"And whoever poisoned you could easily find you."

"Well, yes, there is that." She tried to smile but gave up.

"Of course, they know where I live, obviously."

He looked down at her hand, reached his hand out, dropped it back to his side. "Yes, they do. Malcolm has beefed up security, but that doesn't seem to matter."

"Did he report this to the police?"

Gabriel shook his head. "I honestly don't know. I'm trying to keep you safe without overstepping the boundaries."

Her smile was real this time. "You're a gallant man."

He exhaled a breath. "I'm not that gallant. I'm chasing a story. But I will honor my obligations to our original agreement."

"Of course you will." She shouldn't feel so disappointed that he didn't declare he'd protect her, no matter the challenge. After all, the man was here to do a job. And she obviously didn't have any business thinking of him in any other way. Especially not in a "please grab me and hold me in your arms" way. After the story he'd told her of the beautiful Adina, was it any wonder the man didn't want to get emotionally involved?

He finally touched a finger to her right arm, the brush of his nearness rasping across her hot skin like a warm kiss. "Lara, you know I'd do anything for you."

She could only nod. She didn't know anything, anymore. "I hear something else in your declaration."

He shuffled his feet, lifted his hand away. "I... we...need to focus on this situation. You're in danger. How many times do we need to tell you that?"

"If you want to leave, Gabriel, go ahead."

"I don't want to do that," he replied, his frustration making his eyes go darker. "I want to help you. I...admire you and your work here, and I get how important it is that you finish what your husband started. But some things are too costly to continue."

Falling for him would certainly come at a high cost.

She swallowed, tried to stay awake. The medicine the paramedics had given her should be kicking in, but she still felt light-headed and on fire. "I want to continue because I have to keep moving, Gabriel. I...I've stayed busy since the day they buried my husband. I have to do this, for him."

"For him, Lara? Or for your own sanity?"

A single tear slid down her face. She should tell

Gabriel everything, but she was so tired and she wasn't thinking clearly. "Both, I think."

"In spite of the danger?"

"Maybe because of the danger. I can't be a coward. I'm not wired that way. When I married into a royal family, I knew the protocol, knew the risks. And I pledged to uphold the standards of the Kincade dynasty. I won't change now."

He finally sank down on a footstool, his masculinity clashing loudly with the fringed bottom. "Then we go on with things. You go ahead with the gala and we watch and wait. I think whoever is behind this will be frustrated by you not retreating. They'll show up that night and make a move. And when they do, we need to be ready."

"I'm ready," she said through a soft yawn. "Ready to find out who's after me. Ready to get back to my quiet, boring life."

He got up and took her hand in his again. "I can see that." Then he leaned down and gave her a quick brush of a kiss on her forehead. "Rest, Princess. I won't leave you, I promise."

Lara drifted off into a sweet sleep, that promise echoing over the terror surrounding her.

Gabriel finished making another grilled-cheese sandwich, this one for Deidre. Apparently the entire staff was starving and no one wanted to call for takeout. Too afraid of being poisoned.

So here he stood in the kitchen with Malcolm,

Deidre and several security guards, all eating the Gabriel Murdock Special.

"It's the only thing I know to cook," he said when he handed Deidre her sandwich. Sourdough fresh from a nearby bakery, cheddar so sharp it fairly sliced at the buttered bread and a big iron skillet. "Now if you all don't mind, I think I'll make myself one of those."

Malcolm grinned, then took a long swig of his water. "I have to say, this is a mean grilled cheese, Mr. Murdock."

Gabriel nodded. He thought maybe softening up the staff might lead to a better understanding of the dynamics of this household. "Malcolm, I told the princess I'd stay right here tonight, but tomorrow morning, I suggest we head to police headquarters to reexamine the voodoo doll and the miniature Benoit."

"Why?" Deidre asked, her sandwich in midair.

Gabriel shot a glance at Malcolm, then back to Deidre. "I'd rather not say right now. Might be nothing." He'd studied both in his files, but he needed to see the real things to be sure.

"You don't trust me, do you?"

Gabriel stared across the stove at the girl. "I didn't say that. But so much has happened I'd rather not tip my hand. I only want to look at the items again."

"You think there might be more there?" Malcolm asked.

"Yes, I do." Gabriel finished browning his sandwich, flipped it onto a plate and grabbed an apple. He chose to stay on his side of the wide kitchen counter while he sliced the fruit. No, he wasn't in a trusting mood right now.

"I'll go check on Princess Lara," Deidre said, pushing her half-eaten sandwich away. "Thank you for cooking."

Gabriel watched the dejected woman stomp away, then glanced back at Malcolm. "That one is hard to read."

"Yes." Malcolm munched on his bread crust, then with a flick of one hand, sent the other guards packing.

Glad he'd seen one guard outside Lara's door and another patrolling the upstairs balcony, Gabriel leaned over the counter. "Anything else I need to be aware of, Malcolm?"

Malcolm slung a glance over his shoulder. "Deidre told you about her brother, right?"

"Uh-huh."

"That one was sure trouble. Left the girl rather skittish and scared. He was a rebel—got into all sorts of trouble. Tried to involve her in some of his schemes. That's why she left Europe."

The brother kept coming back up. Gabriel made a note to check on him, too. "And you're telling me this because...?"

"The brother knows Deidre is in New Orleans now. He's supposedly clean now, but one can't be sure."

"Interesting. Do you have thoughts on this?"

Malcolm took a long swig of the coffee Gabriel had made earlier. "I do. I'm wondering if the brother isn't somehow involved in some of the nefarious happenings around here."

"Is he dumb enough to try and steal the Benoit?"

"He just might be," Malcolm said with a bobbing of his head. "Bad news, but crafty. He's a grifter and a con artist—or at least he once was. Deidre keeps telling me he's changed, reformed now."

"Deidre mentioned him, in a way that almost seemed like an excuse or a confession. Or perhaps a warning."

"If he's pulling her strings, she'd try to warn us without betraying his trust. If she was trying to run the other day, it'd be because she doesn't want to do his bidding."

That made perfect sense, Gabriel thought. "Oh, like a passive-aggressive type of warning. She's scared of the police because of what her brother's been through. Or she's scared of her brother but afraid to warn us about him?"

"Exactly. She won't rat him out, but she'll give off signals loud and clear. She wants no part of her brother's deeds."

Now they were getting somewhere, Gabriel thought. "For example, if the man she saw on the upstairs balcony happened to be her brother, then she'd warn him away before she screamed and came out of her room?"

"Yes."

"What's the brother's name, Malcolm?"

"Half brother," Malcolm corrected. "Connor Randall. Or at least that's his latest alias, from what my sources tell me."

Gabriel let out a breath. "Connor Randall is here, Malcolm. And I have the pictures to prove it."

Malcolm looked sheepish. "I can't lie to you, then. I'm aware he's here, Gabriel. But I can't tell you why."

The dream moved over Lara with slow-motion accuracy, her mind reliving her husband's laughter and his death. But then things changed and she was staring up at the Benoit. The people seemed to come alive in front of her eyes, moving and laughing and waltzing through the trees. The shepherd looked down on the people gathered in the lush, open field. The flowers glistened; the water rushed downstream; the trees waved against the wind. She could feel the wind on her face. She saw Theo walking toward her, his hand out.

"Theo?"

He touched her, tried to give her something. Lara slung her hand out. The man turned and left.

She called to him, but the words didn't come out of her mouth. Then she heard another voice.

"Lara, I won't leave you, I promise."

Gabriel, calling her back to reality.

She woke up, her eyes flying open. The room

was spotted with gray-white beams of moonlight. She heard a rustling in the chair by the bookcase. "Deidre?"

A masculine cough. "It's me."

Gabriel, here in her room. "What are you doing?"

"Watching out for you."

She lifted up, peeked from the covers. "I pay people to do that, you know."

"Yes, I've noticed. There is a guard at your door and one out on the balcony."

"So why aren't you across the house getting a good night's sleep?"

"I couldn't sleep. I've been going over everything."

"Did you find something?"

He got up and came to stand near her. "Nothing for you to worry about. How do you feel?"

"Better, I think." She ventured up a bit and when the room remained intact, she sat up against her pillows. "Is there any water?"

"Yes, right here." He went to the nightstand and turned up the glass that covered the small crystal water jug. After pouring her the water, he sat on the bed and helped her take a sip. "More?"

She nodded, drank half the glass. "That's plenty." She had a vague memory of this very same thing happening. Someone handing her water and a pill, maybe?

Gabriel fluffed the pillows and pulled her covers

up over the loose dressing gown Deidre had helped her put on earlier. "Are you hungry?"

"Oh, no." She waved that suggestion away with her hand. "But I am wide-awake now."

"I can go if you need some privacy."

I need you.

That realization terrified her. How could she possibly think that, when she'd just dreamed about her husband?

But he's gone. Dead.

She pushed at her hair. "I need a brush." That was something to keep her occupied at least.

He went to her vanity table, felt around and brought back the requested item. But he held it away when she reached for it.

"Let me."

Not what she'd had in mind. And certainly not what she'd expected from a man like Gabriel Murdock. Not at all.

"Okay." She swallowed again, her throat constricting against the piercing pain forming in her heart.

He sat down on the bed again. "Turn your head."

She turned her face away, glad he couldn't see the truth in her eyes. Gabriel started brushing her hair, the feel of the bristles moving over her scalp a delicious diversion and a tormented joy. "That feels so nice."

He finished and put the brush down on the nightstand. His next words were husky and full of a gentle tremor. "Anything else, Princess?"

She lowered her head, tried to avoid this temptation. "No, thank you."

But Gabriel didn't like that answer. He turned her around, lifted her chin so he could see her there in the moonlight. "Are you sure, Lara?"

She didn't speak. Instead she leaned against him and accepted his embrace as he reached around her and tugged her close. "It's okay," he said, holding her, his hand moving through her hair. "It's okay, Princess."

She wanted to believe that, but the dream kept shouting at her, playing over and over in her mind.

She allowed herself this one indulgence, the need to be held in a man's arms. In his arms. Then she asked God to provide her with the strength to see this through, no matter what.

After a while, she lifted her head and looked up at him, knowing she could trust this man with her worst fears and her deepest secrets. Maybe God had sent Gabriel here to help her find the truth, to expose those secrets and to finally bring her some peace. Maybe she could help him to heal, just a little.

So she cleared her throat, wiped her tears and braced herself for what was to come. Then she spoke. "I think my husband might have been murdered."

THIRTEEN

Gabriel sat back on the edge of the big bed. "What makes you think that?"

How could she explain this? She'd never once voiced it, but now she felt as if Gabriel was the one person she could tell. But speaking it after harboring her fears all these years left her shaky and unsure.

"My husband was an expert marksman, an avid hunter who abided by all the rules and regulations. What they say happened—I just never could picture how someone could mistake my husband for a deer, even if he did blend in with his surroundings. But I was told the deer were heavy in the woods since it was the beginning of hunting season."

Gabriel gave her a direct glance. "I did research while I was waiting to hear about you. Are you sure his bodyguards saw what happened?"

"According to the official report. He always had bodyguards around. They claimed he was walking up a hill near the lodge and another hunter saw movement and thought it was a deer. They heard a shot, ran to protect Theo, but it was too late. He fell down right in front of them. They were unable to revive him."

"And you don't believe that?"

"No. The shooter used a high-powered rifle with a scope." She sat up and tugged her dressing gown close, swallowed back her tears. "At first, I accepted the official report, but then when I'd had time to think about things I started doubting what I'd been told. He could have easily zoomed right in on my husband."

"And are you telling me everything now?"

"I want to be completely honest."

Gabriel nodded his head for her to continue, but she still couldn't voice all of her fears. This was too dangerous.

When she didn't say anything, he asked, "Could it be that the people around him are lying?"

"His bodyguards might have tried to protect him, but they both swore it was an accident, pure and simple. They were witnesses, Gabriel. They reported that the friend who accidentally shot Theo was devastated."

She closed her eyes, remembering the funeral, remembering her husband and remembering how the friend who'd accidentally killed him had tried to stand by her and help her. Had she been a fool?

"That friend went through as much grief as I did, or at least I thought that. He left the area and went back to France. I haven't seen him since the accident."

"Frederick Cordello? He might have been faking it."

Lara shut her eyes. Gabriel was so close to the truth. "He kept telling me how sorry he was. There was an official investigation and he was cleared, but his reputation was ruined, all the same."

"What do you know about him?"

She inhaled, hating the sick feeling in her stomach. "Frederick? He's the heir to a vast fortune, mostly acquired from various titles and estates all over Europe. He and Theo grew up together, went to school and university together. I could never have imagined him hurting Theo…or shooting his best friend."

"People can surprise you."

She nodded, pushed up and over the side of the bed. Should she confess her plan? No, not yet.

Gabriel took her arm. "What do you need?"

"A shower and some soup. And to finish this conversation."

He gave her a once-over glance. "Do you want me to call Deidre?"

"No. If you'll go make the soup, I'll get dressed and meet you downstairs."

"Are you sure? You still look pale."

"Moonlight will do that to a person."

He smiled, tugged her close. "You have to be the most positive person I've ever met." Then he stood there, holding her. "But I agree this conversation is not over, Lara. You can't tell me something like that and then demand soup."

She wished she'd kept it to herself, but now that it was out there, she had to trust him to do the right thing. She would have to tell him everything, sooner or later. But not tonight. "I told you that because I'm afraid whoever killed Theo is now after me."

He let her go, stood back to inhale. "So you've known all along that this was serious. Deadly serious."

"Yes." She took a couple of steps, glad she could stay upright. "The voodoo doll had a tiny emblem embroidered on her skirt."

He stalked in a circle. "A fleur-de-lis? Did it have the initials UN on it?"

"No initials, but yes, a fleur-de-lis. So tiny I hardly noticed it at first. It was a few stitches near the bottom of the yarn."

"I never saw that," Gabriel said. "But I've been studying the Benoit and one of the women in the picture is holding a straw basket with a fleur-de-lis on it and the initials UN. I think it means *one*."

"The first one," Lara added. "Let me get a shower and I'll explain everything."

Gabriel hated the truth of betrayal, but his whole view of this place and this princess had been knocked off its foundation. She'd been holding back the whole time. And here he'd been worrying that Lara didn't trust him when she was the one who couldn't be trusted.

You wanted a second chance, he thought. *That's why you were so ready to rush in and play the hero.* What if he failed again?

He thought of Adina's dark, laughing eyes. Had she died because of him? He prayed God wouldn't let him make the same mistake here.

He stirred the tomato-basil soup and waited, his mind whirling with tidbits and memories. Had Lara known who was chasing them that night? And maybe Lara even knew about Deidre's brother. Did she know he was the man Gabriel had spotted with the reporters? Maybe she'd even known where Herbert was hiding out. Too many questions.

He stirred the bubbling soup, then glanced up to find Lara standing in the wide doorway from the hall. "How are you?" he asked, telling himself he wouldn't let these erratic feelings he had for this woman cloud his reasoning. He'd never once gotten this involved with a subject, not even when he'd tried to help Adina. Had he been duped?

"I know what you're thinking," she said, her hand against the wall.

"Princess, you have no idea what I'm thinking." He turned off the soup and poured some into a large mug, then placed the mug and some crackers on the counter with a glass of water and a spoon. "Should I test the food for you?"

"Don't be ridiculous," she said, taking a slow step toward the nearest chair.

Chivalry overrode indignation. Gabriel went to her and helped her into the chair. "You should have stayed upstairs."

She gave him a steely-eyed glance. "I needed to be up and about. I dismissed the guards. They need sleep."

"And you don't?"

"I'm exhausted, yes," she said, her gaze wandering. "But I've been exhausted since the day my husband died."

He stood there, seeing in her eyes what he should have seen all along. Then it hit him. "I just realized what you're trying to tell me. I understand everything now. You kept telling me you had to see this through—the gala in the Quarter, building the houses here in New Orleans. I think I've got it now, Lara."

"And what do you see?" she asked on a whisper of fear that hinged on that determined look in her eyes.

"You didn't come to New Orleans just to honor your husband's legacy. You came here to find his killer, didn't you?"

Lara let out a breath. "Yes. But you're the only one who knows that, and I'd like to keep it that way."

Surprise etched his face. "I'm honored that you decided to trust me. I mean, really trust me."

Lara hated withholding things from the people closest to her. She couldn't explain all of the details to Gabriel, not yet. "I had to be sure, Gabriel. At first, I didn't divulge my suspicions to anyone on my staff. This is why I only brought a few trusted people with me. They know some of this, but I was afraid to involve them, since I can't be sure who is behind this attack. But only you and I know what I just told you, and as I said, I'd prefer—I insist— that we keep it that way."

Gabriel did a quick visual of the kitchen and the hallway. "In this house? Near impossible."

She shook her head, silent for a minute. "I don't trust anyone now. I thought I'd brought in the perfect team but—"

"But after you've been threatened, shot at, run off the road and poisoned, I'm thinking you realize that's not the case."

"You're my only hope, Gabriel. Can I count on you to help me see this through?"

She waited for his reaction. Would he bolt out of here and leave her to do this on her own? Or had God sent this man to team up with her and finally end this nightmare?

Silence ticked away right along with the grandfather clock in the foyer. "Gabriel?"

"I won't leave you, Lara."

She sighed again, nodded. "I will continue, with or without you. But having you here will make me feel better."

"You mean, now that I've been caught up in the thick of things? Now that I've shown you I can be trusted?"

"You must understand it's hard for me to trust anyone these days."

"I get that. And I even get that you couldn't blurt this out when we first met. But you need to understand, I don't like being used."

"I'm not using you," she replied. "You stumbled into this, but I thank God you came when you did. At first, I didn't want a photojournalist following me, but after reading over your credentials, I decided you might be exactly what I needed. I've prayed for an ally. I believe I've found one in you."

"And yet you couldn't tell me this right away."

"I didn't think anything like this would happen," she admitted. "I planned to do my own investigation since the accident with Theo happened in the States." She put a hand to her collar. "Then when I started being harassed and attacked, I knew I was onto something. Someone wants me dead, too, before I find out the truth."

He didn't seem convinced. She really couldn't blame him for being skeptical. It wasn't in Lara's nature to lie or withhold information. But she had to protect her husband's legacy.

"I want the truth to come out," she finally said. "Someone else could have killed my husband, and Frederick might have taken the fall. He's ruined now, disgraced and vilified. He had to retreat to one of his estates. He's never seen in public anymore."

"But you still believe he was wronged?"

"I don't know. Frederick insisted he saw a deer."

"Even looking through the rifle's sights?"

"Even so. I read over all the reports."

Gabriel took a sip of coffee. "That would have to be some kind of setup. Making sure your husband was in a certain spot, making sure Frederick was in another spot. Somehow showing a deer, real or imagined, in the woods." He set down his cup. "Where in Louisiana did this accident take place?"

Lara took a deep breath. "A couple of hours north of New Orleans, on a private hunting reserve."

His surprise changed to doubt again. "Now we have another possible suspect for attacking you— Mr. Cordello. I guess he's not invited to your party."

Lara lowered her gaze. "Not officially." But she knew Frederick would show up. He was bitter about being shunned and exiled, and he wanted her to acknowledge him in public to end the speculation. "We kept the details of the accident out of the press as much as we could. For a long time, I didn't even know where Theo had been killed." She stared down at her lukewarm soup. "At first, I was too distraught to think about anything except how much I loved and missed my husband."

She didn't miss the tightening in Gabriel's expression. She wouldn't lie about her deep love for Theo, but today, sitting here with this man, she wished she'd kept that to herself. Why did Gabriel make her heart feel so treacherous? Maybe because he was the first man since Theo who'd made her stop and wonder about her future? Maybe because she was so attracted to Gabriel?

He stood there staring across at her, his eyes dark with swirling questions. "You've had your pretty head in the sand, Princess. If you've suspected this from the beginning, why haven't you come forward before now?"

Lara had to tread lightly on this. "I'm the widow of a prince. I have a title, yes, but when you get right down to it, I'm a commoner who married into royalty. I don't have much say in the overall dealings of my husband's dynasty."

"A gilded prison? A paranoid princess?"

"Don't be so dramatic, Gabriel. I come and go as I want, but I have to do things within reason. The only reason I'm here now is because the powers that be think I'm here doing good work for the Kincade Foundation—and I intend to continue with that plan, since I believe in the cause. We must uphold that name above all else. If anyone knew my real reason for being here, I'd be carted off to a remote estate, and I'd be told to keep my mouth shut. We can't have a scandal. My husband's remaining relatives would rather see me dead than have me take any more of their massive holdings. For all I know, it could be one of them."

"You're in the center of a big conspiracy," Gabriel

said, his tone hinging on disbelief. "This is more than a story. It's a major event—full of mystery and espionage, and of course, it involves a beautiful princess and a priceless painting. The stuff of dreams."

Lara got up and held on to the table. "You sound skeptical and I expected that. It's part of the reason I kept things from you. That and the fact that I don't owe you any explanations. This is my life. And I've had to be my own advocate regarding certain aspects of this life. Rest assured, Gabriel, I've been quietly investigating this for a long time now. I don't need you to tell me what I've done wrong or that in spite of all of this, I'm still blessed. I want to do the things I came here to do. I want to help others. But I also want to find some peace of mind regarding my husband's death. And I can't find that until I know the truth."

He stepped toward her, reached out and held her steady. "I want the truth, too. I can get the right pictures, and I can record you in black-and-white or in living color. But I have to have the truth behind the pictures to complete the story." He stopped, took in a breath. "And as much as I want this story and the truth, Lara, I will walk away if you're still holding out on me. I won't put you or myself or anyone else in danger without having all the facts."

"I don't have all the facts," she said, her whisper of a lie grating through her. "I need you to help me find them. Can you do that, please?"

He tightened his grip on her arms, his fingers pressing into her skin with a warmth that sizzled through her. "I can and I will. But only if you can tell me everything you know. We need background information. We need facts. And we need to find out why the Benoit seems to be at the center of this."

"I can help you with all of that," she said. "I can even explain about the Benoit. I believe I have all the answers, and now that you're willing to help me, I think we'll be able to end this once and for all."

He leaned close, his dark eyes rich with intent. "Whatever happens now, we won't be at the end of anything, Princess. This will be a new beginning, maybe one where we get to write the script. Just be prepared for that, too, before you bring me along on this journey."

Then he lifted her chin and gave her a soft, sweet brush of a kiss. But that brief encounter held a lifetime of promise.

FOURTEEN

Lara finished her soup and tried to stand, but her feet didn't seem to work.

Gabriel grabbed her into his arms. "You're still weak."

"You noticed." She smiled up at him. "Let's go out into the sunroom."

"Can you walk?"

"I think so."

"Lean on me." He put his arm around her waist.

Lara told her heart to stop beating so hard. Every now and then, a shot of fire pulsed through her veins, reminding her of the adverse reaction she'd had to the food she'd eaten. She couldn't remember mushrooms ever making her feel this way, but that had to be it since she wasn't allergic to anything else. Except codeine.

Had someone put that in her food?

She had a vague image of a man holding out two pills and telling her to take her medicine. Malcolm? Gabriel?

Gabriel settled her in a big wicker chair by one of the wide windows that looked out onto the back garden. "How's that?"

"That's good." She wouldn't say anything about the possibility of codeine right now. Gabriel had enough to decipher as it was.

Lara adjusted her pillow while Gabriel brought over a soft fleece blanket. "You must come in this room a lot. I see books and magazines all over the place."

She glanced around, memories flooding her mind. "It's one of my favorite rooms in the house. So sunny and you can't complain about that view."

He did a scan of the back garden. The tall, lush magnolia trees were beginning to bud. The crape myrtles were already popping with hot-pink and silky white blossoms.

"I don't like it."

"The view or being here with me?"

"The danger. You're vulnerable here."

That was certainly an understatement, Lara thought. Each time she looked at him, she was extremely vulnerable.

"I need to see the sunshine, please."

He sat down on the settee that faced the window, his gaze constantly sweeping the yard. "Okay, so explain about the Benoits."

Right down to business. Lara accepted that he was still angry with her. "You recall when I told you the story of the Benoits—that supposedly there were three of them?"

"Yes. Do you know where the other two are?"

"No. But I believe Theo did."

He sat up, interest flaring in his eyes. "Go on."

Lara didn't want to speak of her doubts regarding her husband, but she had no other choice. "After he gave me the one for a wedding gift, he talked about the other two. He wanted to own them, too. I think he put out feelers, since he'd often heard the story of the man who originally found the Benoit being murdered. Theo believed whoever murdered that man must have taken the other two Benoits."

"But the one he bought had been hidden away, correct?"

"Yes. The man who discovered them was wise enough to hide the one we have now, reportedly the first of the three. Theo believed he had planned to hide all three paintings in different places, to protect them."

"How did Theo find the one?"

"He had connections." She stopped, took a breath and ignored the fire burning at her muscles and veins. "He knew people who dealt in priceless art."

"The good kind of people or the bad kind?"

"Both, I think." She stared out at the banana trees and palms lining the fence. "I didn't ask Theo about his art finds. If he wanted me to hear about one, he'd tell me. He wanted the Benoit to be a surprise, of course."

"Weren't you curious about how he got it and about the other two?"

"Yes, but I was a young bride, married into a powerful royal family. I didn't want to upset the apple cart. I've changed since then, of course."

Gabriel actually smiled. "I believe you have." Then he searched the yard again. "So do you think Theo knew about the other two and somehow purchased them and hid them?"

"I do." This was the truth of her worst fears. "I think he wanted them so badly, he bought them on the black market and hid them away. Maybe here in New Orleans."

"Now someone wants to find them."

"Yes. I promise you, Gabriel, I don't know if my husband had the paintings. And I certainly don't know, if he did have them, where he might have hidden them."

Gabriel dropped his head, his brow scrunching. Lara could tell his mind was working, trying to put the pieces of her story together. "But someone might be assuming you have them."

"Yes." She swallowed back the mass of worry and fear. "And if Theo inadvertently stole those two from another owner, they'd want their property back. No matter what."

Gabriel stood, paced in front of the window. "So

they'd do anything to find their treasures. Maybe even kill the prince?"

"That's the assumption, but why would they kill him without at least asking him if he had the art-work?"

"Maybe they did interrogate him or maybe they wanted him out of the way," Gabriel replied, whirling to stare down at her. "So they could get to you."

Lara gasped at that notion. "I never considered that. I thought they came after Theo with only the intent to kill him."

"And they did. That, as I said earlier, leaves you vulnerable."

Lara stood, battled the dizziness. "I'm a target. I've always known I might be. Now, with everything going on, I know the time is near for this to come to an end, one way or another."

"And you're willing to make yourself a target just to protect your husband's reputation?"

"Yes," she admitted. "And to find the people responsible for killing him."

"That's too much of a risk, Lara."

She moved toward him, wishing she could make him understand. "Not for me. Not anymore. I have to know. I have to find the truth."

Gabriel looked down at her, his gaze searching her face. "To prove them wrong, or as a death wish so you can finally be with the man you love?"

* * *

Shocked, Lara shook her head. "I will always love Theo. But I don't want to die anytime soon. I truly want to continue rebuilding New Orleans. We promised this city we'd help. Theo was honest about that at least."

Gabriel wondered what else Theo had lied about or withheld. Maybe the Benoits were just the beginning. "What else can you tell me regarding the paintings?"

"That's all I know, but most of it is speculation."

He sat back, jotting notes. "So we know one painting exists because it's here in the house."

"Yes."

"And we don't have proof of the existence of the two other paintings, but you think your late husband might have known about them?" He wrote on his pad. "Do you think those calls you've been receiving are connected to this, too?"

She nodded. Gabriel noticed she kept rubbing her arms. "Are you cold?"

Lara glanced up, a look of pain twisting her face. "No, I'm having a residual reaction to whatever caused my allergy."

Gabriel bent down in front of her. "Do I need to call a doctor?"

Lara looked up at him, panic in her eyes. "My medicine?"

"Where is it? Do you want more?"

She shook her head back and forth rapidly. "Codeine. In the samples the paramedics left. Or someone left." She lifted a hand and pointed. "Upstairs."

Gabriel didn't want to leave her so he started shouting. "Deidre? Malcolm?" He got out his phone and hit numbers. He had his finger on the 911 button, but Lara pulled at his hand.

"No. Someone gave me the pills."

Gabriel's heart sank with the force of deadweight. "You think it was codeine and not mushrooms?"

She nodded, her hands moving up and down her arms. "I took another one about an hour ago. I remember someone handing me pills earlier. I thought it was you."

"It wasn't," he replied. "That means someone was in your room. Someone besides the paramedics."

Deidre came running. "What's wrong?"

"She's sick again. Codeine, in her pills. We need to check her room."

Malcolm came in, his gun drawn. Deidre explained, then pulled out her phone. "We need to call—"

"No." Gabriel grabbed the phone away. "She thinks the paramedics gave her the wrong medicine. On purpose."

Malcolm let out a grunt. "We have a private physician. The prince used to call on him, but Princess

Lara doesn't like him. I'll page him." He stopped then turned to Lara, waiting for her approval.

Gabriel glanced at Lara. "Can we trust this doctor?"

She gave him a weak nod. "I think so. He has a bluntness that I find offensive, but he's a good doctor."

"What can we do, ma'am?" Deidre asked, clearly concerned.

"I don't know," Lara replied. "It's like ants biting my insides. My head." She grabbed Gabriel's hand. "My head."

Gabriel pulled her up. "I'm taking her to her room. Maybe darkness will help."

He carried her up the stairs, his pace quickening when she moaned in pain. "Lara, hang on. You'll be all right, I promise."

But he couldn't really promise her anything beyond trying to help her stay safe. Hadn't he learned that lesson with Adina?

Lara had come here on a philanthropic mission that covered a dangerous quest. How could he predict the outcome of any of this?

Gabriel pushed at the open bedroom door and hurried to the big bed and gently laid her against the pillows. "I'll be right back."

He rushed to the bathroom and found a fluffy white bath cloth, then wet it. Then he placed the cool cloth on Lara's forehead. "See if this helps."

She nodded. "I…I feel so dizzy, itchy. Pills are on the table. Only a couple left."

Gabriel searched the bedside table. "Did you leave them here?"

"Yes. That man did."

He looked again, his eye catching something on the rug by the French doors to the balcony. Two oblong white pills spilled against the doorframe. "You must have dropped them," he said. Then he went to clean up the pills. The label didn't indicate codeine, but then all pills looked alike at times. He sank down to check for anything else when he saw something out on the balcony.

Another miniature painting.

Gabriel hurried to put the pills in a safe place. He'd give them to Malcolm to be analyzed. And he'd have to tell Malcolm someone had yet again breached the security measures. The paramedics must have given her one shot and then told her to take the pills later. But what if codeine had been in the food Lara had sampled?

Deidre?

Gabriel had just about ruled out the skittish assistant, but there was the brother to contend with, and apparently he was roaming about New Orleans.

Malcolm? No. The man seemed as stoic and solid as they came. Gabriel had a feeling Malcolm would fall on his sword to save Lara.

Maybe one of the guards? But they'd all been vetted and Gabriel had found nothing outstanding on any of them. But Armond or Cordello could easily plant a mole in this house. And what about Connor Randall? Malcolm had been closemouthed since Gabriel had shown him pictures of the man. Which one of the men wanted her dead?

Gabriel stood and went back to Lara. "Feeling any better?"

She shook her head. "The itching. It's inside my body."

"The doctor should be on his way. I don't know what to do for you."

She stared up at him, her words weak. "Stay with me?"

"Of course." He pulled a chair up to the bed, one eye on the small painting propped against a wrought-iron table about five feet from the French doors.

"Has anyone been up here today besides Deidre and me?"

"The paramedics." Her eyes held his. "Maybe one of them gave me the wrong shot." She closed her eyes. "I remember a man telling me to take my pills."

"You could have dreamed that," he replied, his hand rubbing her arm. "But someone might have put codeine in your food, too."

"Possibly. My reaction to mushrooms usually involves hives and swelling, but not this much itching and dizziness."

Gabriel felt her pulse. "Strong. Are you having any type of palpitations?"

She shook her head. "No. Just itchy and hot."

He heard voices downstairs and breathed a sigh of relief. "Maybe they only gave you enough to make you sick, thinking you'd cancel the gala or at least be taken to the hospital."

She coughed and lay back on the pillows. "So the house would be empty?"

"Yes." Gabriel didn't want to tell her about the painting out on the balcony yet. She'd try to get up and look at it. "We'll figure this out, but, Lara, you might have to stop this right now. You can't keep going like this. Each threat gets worse."

"I can't stop," she replied, a single tear moving down her face. "They killed Theo."

"And they could kill you."

Before she could protest, the door burst open and Deidre rushed in with an older, gray-haired man.

"This is Dr. Thomason," Deidre said to Gabriel.

"Hello." The doctor went right to Lara and started taking her vitals, his tone and demeanor quiet and reassuring.

Deidre glanced at Gabriel then motioned him to the other side of the room. "Malcolm said to tell you the doctor has been researched and vetted. We can trust him."

"Are you sure?" Gabriel asked, watching Lara.

"We have to," Deidre replied. "She's ill, but we all agree it's too dangerous to take her to a hospital. With the press and someone harassing her, we felt she'd be safer being treated here."

Gabriel held up the two pills he'd placed in a tissue in his pocket. "I found these on the floor. They're not marked, but obviously they have codeine in them—maybe oxycodone or hydrocodone."

Deidre put a hand to her mouth. "If she'd kept taking those—"

"—she might have died," Gabriel finished.

Deidre burst into tears. "What are we going to do?"

Gabriel pointed to the balcony. "We have more to worry about."

When Deidre turned around, she gasped again but caught herself before she rushed out the door. "The third Benoit," she said, her tone a whispered shock. "Not the real one but all the same—"

"So you know the legend of the three Benoits?" Gabriel asked.

The young woman nodded her head. "Yes."

Gabriel didn't speak at first. He almost asked her about her brother, but refrained. He'd have to ask how she knew later. Maybe Lara had mentioned this to her. Then he said, "We have to warn Malcolm it's out there. And this time, we're not calling the police."

"I agree," Deidre replied.

The doctor turned to them. "Would you two mind stepping outside while I have a private talk with Princess Lara?"

Gabriel nodded and took Deidre by the arm. "Of course. We'll be right here near the door."

When they stepped out into the hallway, Gabriel

turned back to Deidre. "Where was the guard stationed on the balcony?"

"Princess Lara dismissed him when she went downstairs."

Okay, he could accept that. "So the balcony was empty the whole time she was with me."

"Yes."

"And yet, someone got close to her again."

"Yes, sir."

Did he see guilt or remorse in those big dark eyes? "Deidre, you can trust me. You know that, right?"

"I'm telling you the truth."

He wanted to believe her, but the young girl had been on a high stress level since he'd met her. What was she hiding? If she knew her mysterious half brother was roaming around, why hadn't she and Malcolm told Lara?

He'd get to that later, he decided. Right now they had to make sure Lara was safe and out of danger.

"All right," he said. "We'll have a meeting with Malcolm later. Will you go down to his office and tell him what we've found outside? He needs to move the replica painting to a safe place."

Deidre started past him.

"Oh, and, Deidre, tell Malcolm that we don't need to involve the local police. But we do need to sit down and discuss what we can do next."

"To protect her?"

"Yes. And to stop her from continuing with her plans."

FIFTEEN

"I changed her medication to something without codeine," Dr. Thomason said to the group waiting in an anteroom near Lara's suite of rooms. "And I gave her something to ease the reaction to the codeine. Good thing she realized she'd been given the wrong medication. Could have been much worse."

Gabriel breathed a relieved sigh. The well-mannered doctor seemed to be the real deal. He talked in a slow Southern drawl and explained things as he went along. His manner was abrupt but honest, from what Gabriel could tell.

"Thank you," Deidre said, her gaze darting from Gabriel to Malcolm. "Is there anything else we should do?"

The mustached doctor frowned. "Yes, immediately report to the paramedics who tended to her earlier that they administered the wrong medication. They should have asked about allergies."

No one explained to the doctor that one of them had possibly administered codeine anyway. Or that was the assumption here, anyway, until they could prove differently.

"We'll make sure the responsible party knows what has happened," Malcolm responded.

Gabriel made eye contact with the stoic security guard, a silent agreement that they couldn't trust anyone beyond this room.

"Good," Dr. Thomason replied. "And let her sleep the rest of the day and night. She's exhausted. Keep an eye on her and make her rest until all of the medicine is out of her system."

"We will," Deidre replied.

Gabriel had noticed a subtle difference in the woman's demeanor since this latest incident. She seemed to have settled down and taken control, of both her own faculties and the welfare of the princess. What had changed the hyper assistant? Was she being genuine or putting on a much better act?

None of that mattered right now. After Malcolm asked the doctor for complete discretion and then showed him out, he came back into the small downstairs office at the front of the house where he'd told Gabriel and Deidre to meet him. "I think we can trust Dr. Thomason. He's been the family doctor to both Princess Lara's father and mother and to the late Prince Theo for years. He's on a very high retainer so I don't think he'll mess with that."

"Good," Gabriel said. "Now let's discuss the fake Benoit we found on the balcony earlier."

Malcolm pulled the square, foot-wide miniature

out from behind his desk. "I wouldn't know this from a Monet or a Picasso, but if you think it looks like the Benoit, then we'll start there."

Deidre pulled her glasses up on her nose. "It's very similar to the one in the parlor. I wish we hadn't let the police take the other miniature away."

Gabriel stared at the painting. "This one has water as its theme. The ocean, clouds, rain, the lamenting women standing by the rising river, crying. There's a sadness to this rendition."

"But the shepherds in the sky are similar to the others," Deidre replied. "Watching over their sheep, so to speak."

"Yes." Gabriel did a thorough scan of the painting, searching for anything that might indicate the number three.

Three women stood crying, their hands covering their eyes, exaggerated teardrops blending in with the coming storm.

He searched for a basket such as the one he'd seen in the Benoit in the parlor. Nothing. Maybe he'd been wrong about the clues he'd seen before. But Lara had agreed that *UN* in the first Benoit could mean the number one in French. He needed to see the other miniature.

"I took pictures—of the miniature at the police station," he said. "Of the rendering Lara spotted the other night. It's in my files on my laptop."

"So we can compare?" Malcolm asked.

"Yes." He explained his theory. Grabbing his case from where he'd left it earlier, Gabriel opened his laptop and searched his photo files. When he found the half-dozen images he'd managed to snap before the police had pulled him away the other day, he enlarged a couple of them so they could search the smaller painting.

"There," Deidre replied, pointing. "On that man's jacket."

Gabriel enlarged the image again. "You're right. A fleur-de-lis and the word *deux. Two* in French." The artist had gone to a great effort to disguise the letters, but once he zoomed in on the jacket, the lettering became clear.

Malcolm squinted through his bifocals. "So the princess has number one, and the one the police have is a print of number two. But if they've never been found, how could anyone know what they look like enough to re-create them?"

They all stared at the framed print in front of them.

"Maybe they're guessing. Or they've heard them described," Gabriel said. Had the prince told someone about them? "I guess they might have actually seen them."

They all looked at the miniature again. Gabriel tracked the figures. "Three women, three shepherds…and here…" He pointed to a large oak tree on the right-hand side of the painting. "Three large branches covered in moss."

"But no French word for *three*," Deidre replied.

Gabriel looked yet again. A little boy was near the big tree, his expression full of grief. But he was holding a dark bag. One hand reached toward the great oak.

"A moss gatherer," Gabriel said, pointing to the bag. And there it was—a tiny red fleur-de-lis with the word *trois* on it.

"French for the number three," Malcolm said with a grin. "You might be onto something, Mr. Murdock."

Gabriel nodded but shrugged. "It could certainly mean there are three of the paintings and we have number one."

"But someone wants two and three," Malcolm said. "And they're toying with us to make that happen."

"Or they think the princess has them or at least knows where they are." Gabriel stared at the sad little urchin. "If they can get her to give up her work here and leave, they'd be able to search for the other two."

Malcolm pulled at his mustache. "But why now? She hasn't been back for close to two years. They could have searched the house up and down during that time."

"Maybe they knew the other two weren't here, since the real Benoit was always switched with a print when she wasn't staying here."

"Good point," Malcolm replied. "I didn't even know that until we arrived this time, so how could they?"

Gabriel tapped his fingers on the desk. "They know we have the real number one *now* because of your big event."

Malcolm grunted. "That means this must be someone on the guest list. Do you still believe Louis Armond might be behind all of this?"

"I don't have any reason to accuse him," Gabriel replied, "but he's first on my list."

"That doesn't mean they need to kill her," Deidre said on high-pitched breath. "Why doesn't this person come and talk to her, instead of harassing her?"

Gabriel stared at the print in front of them. "People will go to any extreme for art worth millions of dollars."

He sent both Malcolm and Deidre a scrutinizing glance. "So I suggest if either of you have any information that might help us protect Princess Lara, now would be a good time to tell me about it."

Deidre's brown eyes widened. "You still don't trust us?"

Gabriel didn't miss the flash of a warning that had moved between Deidre and Malcolm. "I'm a good judge of character, and I think both of you care deeply about Princess Lara. But I also think you're both hiding something from her. And that concerns me."

Malcolm let out a long sigh. "He's right, Deidre. Mr. Murdock came here for one purpose, but things have changed. He's gone from being a photojournalist who stays in the background to being in the center of this mystery. I think we need to enlighten the man."

Surprised, Gabriel squared his shoulders and kept his blank face. "Well, I'm listening."

Malcolm sat back in his squeaky desk chair. "As you know, Deidre's half brother, Connor Randall, is in New Orleans."

"Yes, I've already figured that one out," Gabriel replied, wondering if he'd ever hear the truth. "Tell me something I don't know."

Deidre started fidgeting with her hair and jewelry. "Yes, but what you don't know—and what the princess can't know—is that Connor has turned over a new leaf. Because of his past crimes, he's been working for several global agencies to help find and return stolen art. That's one of the reasons he's in New Orleans."

Gabriel couldn't believe what he'd just heard. Nor would he have ever guessed this scenario. "Your brother—the one you were so worried about—is now an informant for the authorities?"

"An asset." The woman nodded, relief rushing through the concern in her eyes. "Right now he's working with the FBI."

"To retrieve the missing Benoits?"

Both Deidre and Malcolm nodded.

"I wanted to tell you, Mr. Murdock," Deidre said, her voice low. "I was so afraid Princess Lara would find out and ruin his cover, I tried to leave so I could warn him. I even told her I was worried about him, but I couldn't tell her the truth and I hated lying to her. So I thought I'd take myself out of the situation."

"But I stopped her," Malcolm said, his hands crossed in his lap. "We're all trying very hard to protect the princess—even Randall. I had to convince Deidre to stay the course so she wouldn't look like a suspect."

"I was so afraid, I rushed out with an empty suitcase," Deidre said, tears forming in her eyes. "Connor knows I'm here, but we can't make contact. He's zooming in on his target, and if I'd warned him, he could have been killed."

Gabriel wanted to laugh, but these people were dead serious. "Your brother is undercover with the FBI, trying to find the missing Benoits?"

"Yes," Deidre replied. "And the only problem is—he thinks Princess Lara is hiding them."

A slow rage pushed through Gabriel. "Surely he's not the one who's been harassing her?"

"No." Malcolm tapped a finger against the arm of his chair. "He's been trying to find out about that, same as us. But he has to be careful. He's traced the paintings to New Orleans, and he's got evidence that the prince had them smuggled back here. So he's been watching the princess to see if she shows any signs of knowing the location."

Gabriel got up to pace in front of the desk. "And why can't Lara know he's doing this? If he sat her down and explained—"

Deidre's words were barely above a whisper. "Connor can only follow the directions from the FBI or risk being sent back to jail. They believe Princess Lara is involved, but Connor doesn't. My half brother is caught in an impossible situation. We all are now."

Gabriel let that soak in. "So he's in on protecting her, even though he's pretending something else entirely? Such as being an employee of Louis Armond Industries?"

"Yes," Deidre said, her breath a shudder. "And I'm afraid for both of them, but I can't warn her. That's why I've been so jittery. It took my brother a long time to reach this point. He's trying to make right on a lot of things. If he makes one wrong move, however, he could go to prison for a long, long time." She started rocking against her chair. "I haven't slept a wink—"

Gabriel held up a hand. "So neither of you know who's been after the princess? Who placed those prints on the balcony, possibly poisoned her food or gave her bad medicine? Someone tried to kill her on more than one occasion. But you don't know who that might be?"

"Connor is checking his resources," Deidre replied. "But he can't talk to me right now so I can't help you there."

"And we're doing the best we can," Malcolm said. "Her Royal Highness insisted we bring a small protection detail. She didn't want to make waves or seem entitled. She wanted to blend in with the people of New Orleans."

"As if that's possible," Gabriel replied. "What will we do if Randall accuses her?"

Deidre started wringing her hands. "Or worse, reports that she could be involved."

"That would be very bad," Malcolm said on a redundant note.

Gabriel still had a lot of doubts. And questions. "Why do you two know so much about Randall's involvement in this?"

Deidre stopped rocking. "I saw him one day in the Quarter. I almost fainted. At first, I was afraid he'd come here to do harm to me or the princess, but he followed me and begged me to believe him."

"Did you verify this?" Gabriel asked Malcolm.

"Yes. I cleared it with the FBI and promised to stay out of things. A promise I sorely regret, since they've done nothing in the way of protection for the princess." He hit a fist on the desk. "They're watching and evaluating. Mainly, they want us to stay out of their way."

"So we're back to square one," Gabriel said, shaking his head. "We have to find out who's after those other Benoits."

Deidre nodded. "And it would be good if we could figure out where they're hidden before anyone else does."

Gabriel decided he'd work on that while Lara was recuperating. "I'm going over the painting here and the two fakes, too. We found the one, two, three hints. The other clues have to be hidden in the paintings."

"Good luck with that," Malcolm said drolly.

"It's a start," Gabriel replied. He grabbed the miniature and his laptop and headed to the parlor to do some more research.

Lara woke up the next morning wondering what had happened.

Her head was foggy with threads of conversations and particles of memories. Then she remembered—she'd been poisoned, probably through her food or with a heavy dose of codeine. Enough to make her have an adverse reaction.

Gabriel. He had been there with her, had helped her, held her. Had he given her medicine, too? Lara sat up and pushed at her hair while she stared at the streams of late-morning sunlight sneaking through the drawn curtains and blinds.

Did she still have guards watching over her?

Getting up, she held on to the bed to steady herself, but at least the itching and shooting pain had both left her body. Searching for the house phone, she called Deidre.

"I'm up and I'm going to take a shower. I'm fine, really. Much better. I'd love a cup of strong coffee and some dry toast, but don't bother bringing it up. I'd prefer to eat downstairs. This room is oppressive."

"You still need to rest," Deidre replied. "Everything is under control regarding our event, but we think we need to find a different caterer, of course. I've been down to the Quarter to go over the agenda for the gala and the silent auction. The Garden Mansion is all set, ma'am. That is, if you still want to continue."

"Of course I want to continue," Lara replied. She wanted to keep at it until she could flush out the person who had murdered her husband. "I'll go over the details with you after breakfast. And... thank you, Deidre."

Lara hurried through a hot shower then dried her hair and put on some fresh makeup. After dressing in a white cotton button-up shirt and a pair of black ankle pants, she felt much better.

Not dressed to suit the multitudes, but comfortable for a change. She could make some calls regarding the construction zone for the new houses that were being built. The construction foreman had already invited her out to see the progress they'd made. That would give her something to focus on.

Something besides worrying about her life and... wondering about her feelings for Gabriel Murdock.

She'd go out to the construction site, if anyone

would be willing to take her. She didn't want to be trapped in this beautiful, old prison, but going out might prove to be dangerous for everyone right now.

Her cell buzzed. When she saw the unknown number, Lara hit Answer. "What do you want from me?"

"I thought you wanted the truth from me. Not much longer now, Lara."

"You...you were in my room. You gave me that codeine, didn't you? I thought you'd been wronged, but I know the truth now."

"You were dreaming, my dear."

The call went silent. But Lara knew she had not been dreaming at all.

She'd come here with every intention of finding the person who'd killed Theo. She'd hoped that discovery would lead her to the two missing Benoits, too, so she certainly wouldn't let that coward win. She wanted to give all three of the infamous paintings back to New Orleans.

To make amends.

But somehow, she'd become caught up in the second part of this mystery. Someone wanted her dead, too.

"I can't let that happen. Not yet, anyway."

Lara marched down the stairs, determination overtaking the dregs of her allergies and the tickling fear centered in her soul. While memories of Gabriel holding her kept rising up out of the fog in her mind, she tried to clear away the dark places so she could put on a good front.

When she reached the bottom of the curving staircase, she saw Gabriel in the parlor, staring up at the Benoit.

Why did her heart suddenly rush ahead of her brain each time she was around this man?

"That is the source of all of my woes," she said as she entered the room. *That and you, right now.*

He turned to her, his smile hesitant, his tone unmistakable. "I can certainly agree with that."

"You look exhausted," she said. "Come into the kitchen with me and have some coffee."

His eyes flashed in awareness and appreciation. "Thank you. Are you sure you should be up and about?"

"I feel much better. Yes, I need to keep moving. I slept, so that helped, but I'm still a bit weak. I'll be better after coffee."

He took her by the arm and guided her into the kitchen. "I see Deidre has everything ready."

Lara let him hold her chair, allowed his hand to brush her arm. Nice to have a man around, someone to talk to, someone intelligent and caring and willing to help her get through this awful time. And yet, she resented the way he made her feel. "Thank you."

Gabriel sat down across from her, his eyes holding hers.

"I have a theory on the Benoits, Princess."

Lara lifted her chin. "I'm all ears."

"First, someone left another small print on the balcony. Outside your room this time."

"Another breach in my security." She should be shocked, but she had already figured out *he'd* come to her room. "Where is it?"

"In the parlor with the painting. I want to compare them with a photo I managed to get of the first print we found."

"All right. And then you'll explain your theory?"

"Yes. Nothing to help us find the other two, but a start."

She wished they could find the others. If she could find the Benoits, she could get on with her main goal for being here: pinning down the person who'd murdered Theo. The very same man who'd given her those pills last night.

SIXTEEN

"I can see it now."

Lara glanced from the painting hanging over her fireplace to the one Gabriel had placed on the coffee table. Then she took another look at the one he'd enlarged from an image on his computer.

"*Un, deux, trois.* One, two, three."

Gabriel's gaze followed hers. "So the legend of the three Benoits might not be a legend, after all. Just as you suspected, it could be true."

Glad to have something concrete to think about, Lara kept studying the paintings. "Did you notice the other pattern?" She pointed to the portrait. "In this painting, there is one of everything. One woman carrying a parasol, one gentleman strolling behind her. One dog and one little girl running after the dog." Then she pointed to the basket. "And the single woman with the basket." Together, they looked like a group of people strolling along the riverbank. But when she separated them out, they all looked a bit lonely and isolated in spite of the lush surroundings. That image resonated with Lara because it was exactly how she'd felt when first returning to New Orleans.

Gabriel came to stand by her, the clean, soapy scent around him clouding her rational thoughts with his nearness.

"One oak tree, one boat out on the river, and in the dream above their heads, clouds and cherubs, but only one shepherd guarding them."

"Christ." Lara couldn't help the lump in her throat. "I never stopped to consider." A fierce warmth filled her heart. "He's been watching over this house and me and I never saw it, no matter how many times I stood and studied this painting." She turned to Gabriel. "He sent you, I believe. God always places people in our lives for a reason."

She had to hide the real question screaming inside her head. Had God sent Gabriel to protect her, or to stop her from doing something she might regret the rest of her life?

Gabriel's dark eyes held a depth that was hard to read, but Lara let that depth wash over her as they stood side by side. "It's the same with the two prints. Look here at number two—two of everything. Two women picking cotton, two men feeding the animals, two children playing with two wooden toys." He went on to show her number three. "The clouds and cherubs are still there. But one shepherd in the first, two shepherds in the second and three in the third."

"Shepherd angels. Maybe representing Christ, Christ and God, and the Father, the Son and the Holy Ghost. The Trinity."

"We're close, Princess," he said, his warm breath tickling against her neck. "So close to breaking this down."

"Yes, I think we are."

Gabriel put his hands on his hips. "Someone has seen the other two. They must have, to have managed to re-create them."

"Or they're doing this to confuse me," she said. "But if these paintings are out there, we have to find them first."

They stood there for a long moment, an awareness wrapping around them like soft netting, tugging them together. Lara wanted to speak, to tell him how much she appreciated him. She leaned in toward him. He moved an inch closer to her.

They heard a rustling behind them.

Lara shot away from Gabriel. "Deidre, is something wrong?"

"No, ma'am." Deidre gave them both a knowing smile. "We've received several RSVPs. When you're feeling up to it, we should finalize the plans. Only a few days now."

"Of course," Lara replied. "But later today, I might ride over to the construction site." She shrugged when both Gabriel and Deidre gave her a shocked look. "I'll take Gabriel with me so he can get some preliminary shots. And Malcolm can follow with his men. I need to get out of this house."

"You're supposed to rest," Gabriel warned.

"I have rested. But I've been promising the construction foreman I'd come for a tour—without the media. Can we possibly arrange that?"

Deidre glanced at Gabriel. "Yes, if Mr. Murdock is with you."

"I see you've won her over in my absence," Lara said to Gabriel. Deidre did seem a lot more settled than normal today.

"I'm trying." He gave her that long, appraising look again. "I agree with Deidre. You have to be careful. Malcolm has interrogated the caterer, and he's having the food from yesterday tested. You need to consider another caterer, if that's possible at this late date. No matter what the head caterer says about food safety and quality, someone might have put drugs in your food. And that's the likely result, since Malcolm received a full report from the paramedics. The shot they gave you wasn't codeine. But, Lara, they said they didn't leave any pills. You would have had to consult with a doctor for that."

"But…I saw the pills on the table. I took one. Someone told me to take one."

"Did the paramedics leave any instructions?" Gabriel asked. "Did you see them leave the pills?"

"I don't remember. I was in and out and everything was foggy. Someone handed me a pill and a glass of water." Maybe she had dreamed that. "I think someone else came into my room. I thought it was you."

"And I found two pills on the floor by the balcony doors," Gabriel replied. "We don't doubt you. But someone must have brought those pills to you after the paramedics left."

His look of distrust encompassed both Lara and Deidre. Did he doubt Lara now, too? "That would imply someone who works here is the culprit," Lara said. "We've gone over that and cleared everyone. So I believe whoever left the painting on the balcony also must have left those pills."

"We don't know how the pills got there," Deidre said, her tone shaky now at best. "We've verified all the guards were in position. It's unexplainable."

Lara was beginning to wonder if she'd misjudged the people she'd hired to help her. Everything that had happened had occurred when her immediate staff members had been in the house. Could one of them be trying to scare her away? Had one of them figured out her plan for the gala? Or maybe one of them was helping her tormentor?

She could at least be honest about one thing. "I'm beginning to understand why all of this is happening. Someone else knows there were three Benoits, and they obviously think I have all three."

"And that's why you need to be extremely careful," Gabriel warned. "Especially at the gala. Are you sure—"

"I'm not canceling the gala and that's final," she retorted, her halfway-good mood going dark. "If I do that now, they win. And it will look suspicious, as if I'm the one hiding something. I hope to bring this to light by observing everyone who comes through our receiving line."

Another look passed between Gabriel and Deidre.

"Whose side are you on, Gabriel? Is there something I need to know?"

"Why don't we finish up what we're doing here, and then I'll alert Malcolm about you going to view the construction site?"

He was hedging. Now what? Lara wondered. For all she knew, he was the one harassing and scaring her. Maybe he'd convinced Deidre to help him sabotage her efforts.

"Deidre, let's go over the RSVPs and get that out of the way," Lara said. Deidre's hovering about was beginning to get on her nerves. Taking a breath, she told herself the girl meant well. Gabriel's suspicions were rubbing off on Lara, too. Or maybe he had planned things to make her suspicious of her staff. "Excuse me, Gabriel. This won't take long."

Gabriel's expression held a hint of frustration. Was he going to hover even more now, too? Reminding herself that he'd saved her more than once, Lara sent up a prayer of gratitude and decided she should stop being a brat about things. She shouldn't second-guess everyone around her. Gabriel wasn't here to harm her.

But if she didn't advocate her own safety, who else would? She had to continue with her routine and keep things as normal as possible. Not in spite of the danger, but because of it. The person harassing her could possibly be the person who'd killed her husband. She needed to lure that person out of hiding. He'd show up. He'd told her so over the phone.

"Check to see if Louis Armond has responded," she said while she watched Gabriel turn back to the Benoit.

Deidre bobbed her head. "Oh, yes. He's definitely coming to the gala. His secretary said he was excited about it being a masked event."

"A what?" Gabriel whirled to frown at Lara. "Masks? Really? That will make it even harder to watch out for you."

"You can watch *and* take pictures," Lara retorted. "It's too late to change that. The invitations went out as such."

"Wonderful." He paced and pivoted. "And Malcolm is okay with this?"

"He's not happy," Deidre said. "But—"

"But he will do as I ask," Lara replied. "I'm not trying to be difficult, and I know I'm in danger. I think we all know that by now. But what better place to flush out someone who might want to do any of us harm? We'll all have on masks, so anyone who veers off course will be noticed right away."

"Or will be able to cover his or her identity."

"We have the names of everyone coming," she said. "I can assure you Malcolm will go over that list and verify everyone on it."

"And yet, you could miss someone. Enemies can easily be disguised as friends."

"That's a good point, Gabriel. I'm finding it hard to trust anyone these days."

They stared each other down, but Lara refused to blink first. Had she been putting all of her trust in the wrong man?

"You'll need a guard standing by the art at all times."

"Check," Deidre said. "Malcolm is vetting extra security for the event."

"And by all of the outside doors. I've seen the venue. That mansion is in the heart of the Quarter. Easy for anyone to come in off the street."

"Check," Lara replied. "Gabriel, we're used to these functions, so we know to have tight security. I agree I have to be diligent regarding my safety, but I also have to go on with my normal routine." She stopped, took a long breath. "If I don't, I'll panic and get as far away from New Orleans as possible. Then what? Do I have to look over my shoulder for the rest of my life?"

He finally caved and glanced away. "No. I have no right to dictate what you should and shouldn't do."

"I appreciate you, all the same."

"But I'm just the photographer, of course." He put his hands on his hips. "I wish you'd take this more seriously."

"I'm very serious," Lara replied, anger overtaking her common sense. "This event is important to me, as you well know."

Did he understand that she hoped to confront her husband's killer at the private affair? That she had an intuition about this? "Can you see my dilemma? If I go on with it, I'll be in danger. But if I cancel it, rumors will swirl, and my attacker will use that to his advantage. He'll realize I'm vulnerable and afraid. I can't let that happen."

"I understand a lot more than you think I do," he finally said. "But we'll have to discuss this later. I'll follow you around, no matter what. After all, I am here to capture you in your best light, but I've also taken on the duty of helping to keep you alive, too."

That little innuendo stabbed at her pride. "I'd expect no less, given that you've been thrown into the middle of this whole affair. I'm sorry for that."

Deidre kept her eyes on the checklist. "Here you go, ma'am."

Lara gave Gabriel an apologetic glance, then hurried through the list. "I see most of our guests have responded. So we'll have a full house."

"Seventy-five by last count."

Lara sat back, going over her own checklist. "We have a solid venue, but I agree I would feel better with a different caterer. Deidre, it's very late in the game and we might have to pay a fee for canceling, but I do think we have to find someone else to handle the food. But be discreet. Don't broadcast the change to anyone, and please have the caterer sign a confidentiality contract."

"I agree with that," Gabriel said, his eyes holding Lara's. "It will be worth the extra expense."

"I'll get right on that," Deidre said, scribbling notes.

"So we have extra security and we'll find another caterer," Lara said, feeling better. "Gabriel will be near me at all times." She stared up at him. "You have the perfect weapon. You have a camera."

"Yes, I do," he said, his tone gravelly. "I always find the answers through my work. A picture doesn't lie, but it can certainly shine a light on the truth."

That sounded like a warning. She couldn't decide if it was aimed toward protecting her, or aimed *at* her. Either way, the man's presence here was an added bonus. Gabriel made her feel safe, but she couldn't let her guard down. Not even with the man who'd come into her world and turned it upside down.

"Someone is lying."

Gabriel heard the anger in Lara's words. "I certainly agree with that. The test came back clean on the food left in the refrigerator, and the paramedics swear they only gave you a mild sedative." He maneuvered the SUV through traffic. "Someone could have switched the food, and one of the paramedics could have received a big payoff for switching your medicine. But how would anyone be able to bribe a medical person so quickly? It makes more sense that someone came into your room either before or after the paramedics left."

"How can we ever prove any of this?" Lara adjusted the baseball cap she'd put on to disguise herself and glanced in the rearview mirror to make sure Malcolm and the entourage were a safe distance behind them. "I tend to believe the paramedics weren't involved, but someone is making it look as if they or someone from my staff is doing this."

Gabriel made another turn. "Well, we've kept the police out of the loop, so we'd have a lot of explaining to do if we bring them back in now. And besides, they're just sitting on that print and the voodoo doll. Chalking those up to overly zealous admirers, last time I checked. They've gone nowhere in finding Herbert or those two men who tried to run us down, either. They can't arrest anyone without probable cause, and who would they go after, anyway?"

"True." She pushed at her sunglasses. "We've questioned every guard Malcolm has hired, several times at that. No one has seen or heard anything, and Malcolm has cameras on each guard station. He'd know if someone left his post."

"And yet, someone keeps getting closer and closer to you."

Gabriel thought about Deidre's half brother again. He couldn't reveal Connor Randall's action to Lara. He'd promised Deidre he'd use discretion. And he surely didn't want the FBI breathing down his throat. His editor would go into cardiac arrest if Gabriel blew this assignment by interfering with a federal investigation.

"Exactly," Lara replied, her head down. "At least we all agreed I could get out of the house for a while."

"Only for a little while. Someone could be watching us right now."

"And thank you so much for reminding me of that."

Gabriel's frown remained intact. "Let's pretend everything is normal and that I'm really only here to get candid shots of you at the construction site. We have a couple of days before you have to worry about the gala. Try to forget all of this while you're away from the house."

"Easier said than done, but I do love that idea. And that's exactly why I needed to get away."

He watched the GPS, then turned once again. "I think we're at the first phase of houses, Princess."

Lara sat back to stare out the tinted window. "I can't believe it's finally going to happen." She looked behind them and then turned back around. "People used to live here, Gabriel. They sat out on their porches and laughed and talked while their children rode bikes and chased each other around the yards. I want to make that happen again. I want this to be a neighborhood again."

"A noble goal, but is this *your* goal or your late husband's?"

"We both wanted this," she admitted. "That's why I have to see it through."

He sat there, thinking of how she'd called out to her husband when she was so ill. "You asked for him, you know. When you were sick. You thought I was him."

Lara took off her sunglasses and peered at Gabriel. "I was confused at first, but then I saw you there. But you left the room, didn't you?"

"Yes. I was back and forth."

"Then you can't be sure I didn't ask for you, too, can you?"

With that, she opened the door and stepped out, her hat over her golden hair, her eyes hidden by the big glasses.

Gabriel grabbed his camera bag and followed. But he had to wonder if she was just playing him. Or if she'd really asked for him during her confusion. Did it really matter? He'd be done with this assignment soon and he'd have to leave. But his fear of history repeating itself sat squarely on his shoulders like a heavy mantle.

He looked up at the cloudless sky and silently prayed a shaky, rusty prayer. *Just let me help her*

survive this big gathering and her work here, Lord.
That's all I have the right to ask of You.
  And of her.

SEVENTEEN

Gabriel walked behind Lara, snapping pictures while she explained the concept of building strong, hurricane-resistant houses. Here, without an entourage, she shined in spite of all the intrigue surrounding her.

"We want to build substantial houses that are eco-friendly, but solid and well made," she said, waving her right hand in the air. "This is the skeleton for the first of many."

Gabriel followed her to an unfinished frame. "Is it two-storied?"

"Yes, but the bottom floor is for storage and a garage. "Building the houses up high will also help if another flood ever occurs. Which we're hoping won't happen, of course, since the levees have been completely rebuilt."

A few workers remained at the site, but since they'd purposely come later in the day to avoid all the hard hats and to throw off the reporters, only a couple of supervisors were here to escort them.

So far, they'd managed to get around the droves of reporters camped out on her street. The police ran them off about every couple of hours, but they always came back. Gabriel and Malcolm had purposely waited until the coast was clear to bring her out the back way.

Gabriel wondered again if one of the people in that crowd was recording and watching for more than just a glimpse of the princess. Any of the ragtag gang camping outside her doors could easily break away and somehow get inside the Garden District compound.

And he hadn't ruled out the infamous FBI informant, Connor Randall, since he had yet to find any background information on the man. Randall must have gone deep to ground. Gabriel fully intended to dig a little deeper into that factor, no matter the FBI or his grumpy editor.

Right now he had *his* ear to the ground and his antenna up to listen and watch for anyone out of the ordinary. So far, so good. Princess Lara was relaxed and animated, a sharp contrast to how she'd felt twenty-four hours ago.

And beautiful. Even in a baseball cap and sunglasses, she looked petite and dainty. Reminding himself he needed to stick to business, Gabriel snapped a couple more pictures and listened to her rapid-fire questions to the construction foreman and his right-hand man.

"So another few days, and I'll hold a press conference here at the site," Lara told the foreman. "Today, I only wanted to see the progress so far. Wonderful job."

They'd reached the end of the street, where a cul-de-sac curved around. Soon, Lara had told Gabriel, there would be houses on both sides of this wide street.

"Homes that will have several bedrooms and at least two baths," she'd said. "Real homes with insulation and air-conditioning and heat, so families can be comfortable. But affordable homes, too. We're making sure of that."

He couldn't deny her dedication. That wasn't an act.

But since she'd confessed that her main purpose here was to "flush out" her husband's killer, he'd had his doubts.

How did she plan to do that? Since she hadn't shared that scenario with anyone, including him, he had to wonder and worry. The woman was in constant danger, but she carried on with a smile. Was she used to being in danger, or was she truly trying to bring the danger out into the open by flaunting herself this way?

She could be a slippery little thing at times, but he planned to continue questioning her until she told him everything.

The sun was beginning to go down past the tree line when the group finally started returning to the vehicles. Malcolm and his detail team had followed them every step of the way, with eyes on each corner of the isolated, deserted property a few miles from the Quarter. Now Gabriel protected Lara on one side and on the other side was Malcolm, who also made sure she had a man behind her. Like a small army, they marched her to the vehicle Gabriel had driven here.

Once they reached the SUV, Gabriel did another visual scan, searching for anyone left on the property or nearby. Using the zoom on his camera, he moved the lens across the perimeter of the housing grid.

And spotted a man on top of an unfinished roof one street over.

Checking around, he noted the foreman and assistant were standing not far from the SUV. Who was the man on the roof?

Gabriel held his camera tight and watched in horror as the man raised a weapon.

"Sniper!" he shouted to Malcolm, his camera clicking away to get proof.

The first shot rang out and pinged near Lara's head. Gabriel pressed her close to the vehicle and pushed her down.

Malcolm came around and hurried to open the door.

"Get in, Your Highness!" Malcolm shoved at her while Gabriel crouched by the door.

More shots zinged through the air.

Malcolm grabbed at his shoulder, but quickly managed to get Lara inside the SUV.

"I've been hit," Malcolm said. Gabriel whirled to push Malcolm down, then called to one of his security team to help.

"Put him inside," Gabriel said while they all stayed low behind the doors to avoid being hit.

Two guards got Malcolm in while one stood with his own gun drawn. He got hit immediately after Malcolm was secured, but his buddies tugged him up and into the vehicle.

"Let's get them out of here," Gabriel called, rounding everyone up.

The construction foreman and his man had managed to get behind the big vehicle but were now trapped. "Get inside," Gabriel called. He opened his door as another round of ammo hit the ground and the vehicle. "We've got to go."

Gabriel hit the gas and urged the big vehicle around the cul-de-sac. The shooting stopped, but everyone in the vehicle started talking at once.

"Take them to the hospital!" Lara shouted. "Malcolm is bleeding."

"Fine, ma'am." Malcolm passed out.

Gabriel took one last look at the tree line and the roofs across the street, but it would be impossible to see the shooter without his zoom lens. At least he'd managed to get some shots in of his own.

Maybe they would finally have a bead on whoever wanted to harm Lara.

* * *

"I can't leave Malcolm."

Gabriel pulled Lara to the side of the big emergency room. "You're too exposed here. Malcolm wants you to go home."

"But he's hurt." One guard had died at the scene. How could she live with herself if something happened to Malcolm? "He's watched over me for years now. I didn't want this to happen. I should have been more careful."

Gabriel's eyes held a solemn knowing. He didn't have to say "I told you so." She felt it in every fiber of her being. Instead, he held her there, his hand pressing against her arm. "Malcolm knows the risks of his job, Lara. He was doing that job. He took a bullet for you. They all did their jobs."

"Yes, and one of them is dead now. I have to live with that and Malcolm being injured. I want this to be over, but I can't stop it now." She didn't realize she'd let that slip until Gabriel's fingers went loose on her skin.

"What do you mean?"

Panicked, she shook her head. "Every day, Gabriel. Every day for the past couple of weeks, I've lived in fear and dread. When will it stop? I can't stop what I came here to do, and yet I'm putting everyone in danger."

"You can stay out of harm's way," he replied, "by going underground and staying out of the limelight. You need to get out of New Orleans. It's not safe for you here regardless of this sense of duty you have about the place."

She moved away then pivoted to stare at him. "This will follow me, I can assure you. And that's the reason I have to finish what I've started."

"Have you been threatened before this?"

"Yes, but in ways I can't explain or prove."

"Lara, you're talking in riddles. Are we talking about your big fundraiser or your need to find your husband's killer?"

"Both," she said on a whisper. "And that's all I can say right now."

Frustration colored his dark eyes in a shimmering rim. "I won't press you now, because I told Malcolm I'd get you safely home once we were through with the police. We've been cleared to leave, so I'm going to take you home now. We've got reporters gathering outside, so we don't have much time before they get the details and plaster them all over the airwaves and the papers. But later, Lara, you will level with me."

Lara's panic turned to anger. "I don't owe anyone an explanation. This is my business and my choice."

Gabriel didn't respond. He guided her through the hospital corridor and informed the guard at Malcolm's door that he'd check on him later. The wound had been a through-and-through that had passed two inches above Malcolm's heart.

Too close, Lara thought. Much too close. Malcolm could have been killed. Gabriel, too, for that matter. They'd flanked her on all sides, protecting her. One of the guards was dead now.

Gabriel took her out the side door and into a waiting SUV. She didn't speak after they were inside, with a guard riding shotgun. But she saw Gabriel glance back at her through the rearview mirror.

Could she trust him to help her finish this? Or should she go ahead with her plan and let matters unfold with no thought for the outcome? What if she canceled the whole event and left New Orleans?

She'd never find the truth and that would destroy her. She had to take one more risk in order to bring things to a final conclusion. She only prayed no one else would have to die because of her stubborn need to avenge her husband's death.

There had always been only one outcome. She had to find her husband's murderer. And she had to do that no matter what.

Please, Lord, help me do the right thing. Help me to end this one way or another. Justice, Father. I ask for justice.

But she was beginning to think that justice might come at a high price.

"I suppose you've seen the papers?"

Gabriel looked across the table at Princess Lara. "Hard to miss. My editor in New York wants in on this story, I'm afraid."

Lara gave him one of those princess looks he

was beginning to recognize. "And of course, you feel obliged to file the real story?"

"I do, but as promised, only if you give me the go-ahead." He leaned up to grab a freshly baked biscuit. "Of course, there seems to be no end to this thing."

"It will end soon."

Gabriel dropped his biscuit. "You scare me. Such finality in that statement. You know, you're messing with some dangerous people. They seem to keep coming."

She looked down at her plate, but not before he saw the hint of secrecy in her blue-green eyes. "I think it will all be over soon."

Gabriel didn't like that statement, either. "What have you planned here, Lara, besides a masked gala?"

"I don't want to discuss it."

"But I told you last night at the hospital I wanted answers." She'd gone straight to her room last night with a request to be left alone.

She ran a finger over the china cup of tea in front of her. "I don't want you involved—I mean, any more than you already are, that is."

He didn't mean to slam down his fist, but when she jumped he realized he'd done just that. "I'm involved up to my eyeballs, according to the local papers. A tire blowout that almost caused a traffic accident, a dead man in an apartment, a car chase across the Crescent City Connection, mysterious gifts dropped off at your supposedly secure mansion, an allergic reaction that almost killed you and gunshots being fired at the construction site. I was there for all of that, Lara. How much more involved can a man get?"

She looked hurt and then angry. "You can leave, you know. I've told you that from the beginning. This isn't what you signed up for, is it?"

"No, but I can't leave you now. You've got me right where you want me, Princess. And you know I can't walk away."

"You mean, not without your story?"

Gabriel got up and came around the table, then lifted her out of her chair. "No, Princess, I can't leave because of you."

He saw a new kind of fear in her eyes. A fear of loving and losing. "I don't know what you mean."

He tugged her close. "Yes, you do. You're a smart woman. Surely you can see it?"

She lowered her gaze. "See what?"

"This," he said, his fingers lifting her chin. "This, Lara."

He kissed her long enough to know that he was in too deep, long enough to feel her relaxing in his arms.

When he lifted away, she pulled back and gasped a short breath. "You shouldn't have done that," she said in a shaky voice. "People are always watching me, as you very well know."

Gabriel didn't care who saw them. He held her

there. "I should have done that the first night I sat at this table, but it's kind of hard to carry on a romance with bullets flying and everyone in this place hiding secrets."

"Please let me go," she pleaded softly.

Gabriel stepped back. "You're playing a dangerous game, Princess. Any other woman would have given up by now, but you seem to welcome the danger. Are you out to prove a point, or are you hoping all the publicity will help your cause?"

Another gasp. This time, in shock. "I can't believe you just said that. If I wanted more publicity, I can assure you I'd find a better way to create it."

"And I can't believe you continue to court danger. You go from crisis to crisis and bounce back with more energy each time. I don't understand."

"I don't expect you to understand."

"Try me," he said, his hand reaching out. He didn't touch her, but he didn't move away, either. "Tell me, Lara. Tell me so I can help you."

She turned to grab the chair, her emotions darkening her eyes to a deep sea-green. "He might be here, Gabriel. That's why I have to see this through. He might show up."

Gabriel's heart zapped with shock. "Who is he, Lara?"

"Frederick Cordello," she finally said. "The man who really did murder my husband, no matter what he says to the contrary."

EIGHTEEN

Gabriel stood back, her confession still ringing inside his head like a warning bell. "But you said it was an accident, that it ruined his life. You said you couldn't be sure, that he took the fall for someone else."

"I thought that at first," Lara said. Looking over her shoulder, then back to him, she motioned Gabriel to the sunroom. When they were inside the open, airy room, she shut the French doors to the main house. "We won't be interrupted here with the doors shut."

Gabriel walked to the row of windows overlooking the back garden. When he turned around, he'd regained control but was beginning to wonder at his own sanity. "I need the truth, Lara. Or I will walk out that door and I'll find the truth and I'll publish it. I have enough pictures to tell this story. I'll find the facts to back it up."

"I don't want you to do that," she said, hurrying

over to him. "You can't. I need you here. You're part of the—"

"—the cover," he finished, disgusted with himself. "Is that why you were so agreeable to having a photojournalist follow you around?"

"No, not at first. Initially, I didn't want you here. I purposely left most of my staff in Europe to protect them. And those who are here know the dangers. But it's been hard on all of us. Poor Deidre almost abandoned me. I don't want you to do that, too."

"They know. Of course they know. It makes sense now that they didn't insist you stop this right away. You didn't tell me they were in on this because you didn't want me to influence them." Anger covered Gabriel in a brilliant red that rivaled the lush roses blooming in the garden. "Everyone but me," he said, the words slicing over the air. "What a complete fool I've been."

"No, Gabriel. I only told Malcolm and Deidre that I expected him to show up and that I would confront him. They agreed to come—they're that loyal, but also because they were concerned he might show up before the gala. And apparently he has."

"Yes, he's here or he's sent someone to kill you."

Gabriel wasn't used to this kind of manipulation. One reason he tried to avoid intimate relationships in his line of work. He couldn't afford to be manipulated because he had to remain neutral in order to tell his stories through pictures. With Adina, he'd fallen hard, but not because she'd tricked him into helping her. Adina had been sincere and scared, afraid of her own family. This woman had apparently calculated every move.

How could he have been so blind?

But he'd lost focus and, apparently, brain cells, too, in dealing with this beautiful princess. And she'd acted the part so well, he'd almost fallen for her. Actually, he *had* fallen for her. That didn't set well in his analytical mind.

"You should have told me this up front, Lara. It would have saved both of us a lot of grief."

"Yes, I should have done that, but I was afraid. I didn't know if I could trust you." Lara stepped closer. "Now that I've met you and you proved yourself over and over, I…I don't want you to leave. You make me feel safe." She did a dainty shoulder lift that might have been a shrug. "I haven't felt completely safe since Theo died."

Still smarting from being used, Gabriel let out a cold chuckle. "Well, I'm glad you feel that way, Princess. I've been on edge this whole time, worrying that I'd have to watch you die. I'm even more concerned about that now."

"You've been in worse situations," she replied, her calmness belying the apprehension in her eyes. "You're a very brave man, Gabriel. Malcolm questioned you and accused you, but he really approved you almost immediately—I think because he sensed an ally in you."

"Look, thanks for the vote of confidence, but I've gone way out on a limb for you. You could have had the decency to tell me what I was walking into. Especially after we found—or thought we'd found—your favorite chef dead."

"I tried." She looked down at the wool floral rug. "I wanted to, so many times. But I decided the less you knew, the better off you'd be. When we found that man dead, I knew Frederick had to be behind this. He always hated how Theo would go on and on about New Orleans food, so he'd certainly heard how fond I was of Herbert's cooking. He knows Herbert. In my own misguided way, *I* was trying to protect *you.*"

Gabriel laughed again. "Protect me? I've been in the line of fire since I walked in this place. Yes, I've been in worse situations, but I was always briefed on what to expect and I was told how to stay out of the way. That's how a good reporter or photographer stays alive." He moved closer to her, his eyes locking with hers. "But here, I was thrust into a dangerous situation, and I had to deal with that because…my first obligation was to protect you. And you knew that. You must have known I'd be obligated to help you." He touched his hand to her face, causing her to look him in the eye. "You figured that out, didn't you? You played on my sense of doing the right thing. And I fell for it."

Her eyes flashed fire. "Gabriel, it's not like that."

"Yes, it is."

He moved away, wondering what to do now. He should gather his things and leave. He had enough material for a good, solid spread on all the work Princess Lara Kincade was doing in New Orleans. He could make it interesting. But when he turned and looked into her eyes, Gabriel knew he couldn't leave.

"Don't go," she said, as if reading his thoughts. "You...you've become very important to me."

"As a shield?"

"No." She stared at him, her eyes luminous with longing. "No, as a friend, as a man I've come to admire and trust. I'll admit there have been moments when I wondered if you weren't in on some of the things going on around here. But there are other moments when I know in my heart you are a good and decent man and you've put your life on the line for me."

Ignoring the pride in her words, he said, "And yet, you still withheld things from me."

She nodded, took his hand in hers. "Now you know the truth. I believe Frederick killed Theo. I believe he paid the two guards a large sum of money to keep them quiet. They both left the service of the Crown, citing grief as their excuses. But I've had them watched. They are not grieving, I can assure you. They're living it up, and I know for a fact their salaries didn't allow for such a lifestyle."

Gabriel became intrigued in spite of himself.

"And Cordello? You said he had to leave, too. Where is he now?"

"Probably here in New Orleans, if my guess is right. But before, he'd been spotted near my home in Europe. I have the pictures to prove it. He's been seen at events where I've been, but he's never once tried to see me, not since the day I told him to leave me alone. He's been watching and waiting and now he's coming for me."

Gabriel didn't like the images that flashed through his mind. He couldn't let this go, no matter how angry he was. He'd have to stay, if only to get to the bottom of this story. "Why is he after you?"

She gave him a hopeful look. "Will you stay? I have to know before I tell you."

He lifted his hand, let it fall to his side. "What other choice do I have, Lara? You obviously know I have feelings for you."

"I…I care for you, too," she admitted. "And I'm glad you'll be staying. I thought I could do this on my own, but now I'm beginning to wonder if I'm in over my head." She stepped closer. "With this threat and with you."

Gabriel took her by the arm to haul her close. "It's sink-or-swim time, Princess. But no more lies, no more secrets."

"I promise," she said. "Frederick is after me because I'm pretty sure my husband had all three Benoits. What I don't know is if he took them from

Frederick and Frederick wants them back, or if Frederick only wants to take them from me out of revenge."

Gabriel sat at a two-hundred-year-old desk in his room and jotted down notes and went over variables. Three people stood out in his mind. Louis Armond, Connor Randall and now Frederick Cordello. Which of the three wanted those paintings?

He called Richard. "Any more word on Connor Randall?"

Richard grunted and protested, but Gabriel knew his editor would be on this juicy puzzle, same as him.

"He is indeed the man your cohorts told you about. He was a criminal, dealt mostly in art theft. But he turned good guy when the FBI brought him in with a 'take it or leave it' offer."

Gabriel chuckled. "Let me guess. 'You help us, we'll save you.'"

"Yep. So if this man is loitering around New Orleans, he's there on the FBI's time to sniff out some sort of artifact or to catch someone who might be about to steal a nice piece of art."

"Or three," Gabriel added. "I wonder where those other Benoit paintings could be. Obviously, they aren't in that warehouse across the river, or Lara would have told us. And I wonder if Randall is here to help or to hinder. He could be putting one over on the FBI."

"You're a smart man," Richard said. "Follow the clues, Murdock."

Gabriel sat up in his chair, his gaze wandering around the guest room on the second floor of the Garden District mansion. A cozy place with its deep blues and rich browns. A nice, comfortable room, but this whole house was full of secrets. He hated secrets. "We did figure out there were three Benoits, based on what we've seen." He stopped, grunted out a sigh. "I can't get why someone would send prints of the other two. But it's like you say— maybe they hold part of the puzzle, something I'm not seeing. I'll go back to the Benoit hanging here in the house."

"Keep me posted," Richard said in his dismissal voice.

Gabriel didn't dare tell his editor that the princess had ideas of her own about how to catch a thief. He'd have to see how that would play out at the upcoming gala. He now believed the gala was a setup, a trap to lure in a killer. And that was why Lara refused to shut down the whole affair and probably why she refused to bring in the police until she had no choice. But how many people knew this? Then there was the other question. Should he let her keep going or should he try to stop her?

Either way, she would be in danger until the person behind these deeds was brought to justice.

He had no other options. Gabriel had to be there with her to see this through. For his work and… for the princess.

"The editorial page is not happy with me," Lara said the next day. "Or rather, the entire paper is full of articles about people who are not happy with me." She looked up at Gabriel and shook her head, relief at seeing him back in her office giving her strength. "They think I'm causing unnecessary violence, that I'm bringing too much attention to the Garden District. My neighbors aren't happy, either."

Gabriel paced around her office, filling the room with an edgy tension. "Well, you've got reporters looking for a story and you've got extra police officers monitoring the perimeters of your home. People don't like this kind of attention."

She watched as he lifted a slat of wood in the plantation blinds and glanced out the front window. They were all on edge with each passing day. Lara wanted this to be over, but she had been taught to see things through to the end.

"Are the reporters still there?" she asked, hoping he'd open up to her. True, *he* was still here. But things between them had gone from warm and caring to chilly and reserved.

He didn't want to be here. She didn't want him to leave here. Not yet. Not until she could breathe again. Or maybe she wouldn't be able to breathe after he left.

"Of course they're still there. They want the truth. But then, we all do."

That little sting hit her in the heart. "I've told you the truth, Gabriel. Can you ever forgive me?"

"Nothing to forgive, Princess. I know the rules. Get in, get the scoop and get out. It's the reporter's creed."

"So you'll honor that creed, no matter your feelings for me."

He dropped the slat and whirled, his dark gaze moving over her. "I'll get the story, in spite of my feelings for you."

She stood and moved her hands down her black trousers. "Well, you won't have to be here much longer. The gala is tomorrow night. Everything is in place, including bringing in police protection for the entire event."

"That makes me feel better," he said, his tone full of sarcasm. "As if that can protect you."

"It's almost over," she said, holding her heart steady. "I only want to get him here so I can confront him, face-to-face. If I can get him to confess—"

"Lara, the man will kill you."

"I can assure you, if Frederick Cordello wanted me dead, I'd be gone by now. He's an expert marksman. There is no way he would have missed yesterday. He's either trying to scare me badly, or he aims to end things at the gala, one way or another."

"Is he also an expert at causing tires to explode and at putting codeine in your food? Or wait, maybe he put codeine pills by your bed and whispered in your ear while you were so ill. Oh, and of course, he's probably an expert at sneaking by guards to leave you all sorts of little presents. Just to mess with your head, of course."

"Stop it," she said. "You've made your point, but as I told you, we've taken extra precautions."

"It's still too dangerous."

She came around the desk, needing to be near Gabriel. "Not if I have you and the others waiting in the wings. I only want to hear the truth from his lips. I want him to confess. After that, I can finally find some peace."

"If you don't get killed."

She stared up at him, wishing she could tell him she thought Cordello was behind all of these assaults. "You think I'm crazy, don't you?"

Gabriel let out a sigh. "Not crazy. Misguided, determined, hurting, yes. But you've thought this through—that's obvious. However, I think you've neglected thinking about how you'll feel once you've found justice. Once that burning goal is over, what then?"

Lara inhaled at the urgency in his words, her heart shouting that her only regret would be hurting him. "You think I'll be left empty after I watch them take him away? After this is over?"

"I worry about that, yes. Without this purpose for revenge that's been driving you, I'm afraid you'll have a lot of regrets." He moved a step toward her. "I'd hate to see that pretty smile vanish forever."

Lara's protective instincts rose up. "You think this smile is real, Gabriel? This smile I put on for the world? This smile that dictates my every waking hour? This smile I give whenever I have to be in the same room with people who loved him and admired him and wanted him to live a long and happy life?" She shook her head, tears burning at her eyes. "This smile is so fake I sometimes find it hard to remember what being happy actually means. I'm tired, Gabriel. So tired. But I have to prove that he killed Theo. My social status is the only weapon I have."

He moved the two steps toward her and took her against him, holding her and hugging her close. "I know you're tired, but you have a lot to live for. There are easier ways to seek justice."

"I can't rest until I know the truth," she said, her head on his shoulder. "I'm so sorry I've put you through all of this. You had nothing to do with what happened between my husband and Frederick."

Gabriel stood back to stare down at her. "What did happen between them?"

Before, Lara would have gone tight-lipped on that subject. But here with Gabriel, all of her defenses were gone. She moved away and went to her desk, then sat down. "They were best friends since boarding school. They did everything together. After I met Theo, we'd all three often be seen out and about. But throughout it all, even after we were first married, I didn't realize that Frederick fancied himself in love with me." She put her head down against her upraised hands. "He resented Theo getting to me first, and he never quite got over that notion."

Gabriel finally sat down. "Did he harass you?"

"No, not at first. It started about a year after our wedding, when he caught me at an event and told me how he felt, told me Theo didn't appreciate me or love me the way he did. It was…awkward."

"Did you have feelings for him?"

"Only as a friend, and honestly, I tolerated him for Theo's sake. They were close, so I ignored Frederick's arrogance and sense of entitlement. I was so shocked I didn't know how to respond. But I let him down gently by telling him I was flattered but I was in love with my husband. I loved Theo. No one else."

She saw the flicker of awareness in Gabriel's eyes. Did he resent her love for her husband, too?

"So he didn't take your rejection very well?"

"No, he didn't. He started sending me gifts and leaving messages. I finally had no choice but to go to Theo." She lifted up again, dark memories swirling in her head. "I think at first Theo wondered which one of us was telling the truth. Rumors of an affair surfaced, but Theo and I had a long talk and he finally believed me. We stood united and showed the world we were happy."

"Then came the hunting trip?"

"Yes. All the time we were married, Frederick didn't just want me. He wanted the Benoit, too. He admired that painting."

She put her hands against her stomach. "He often asked about it. I always thought that was rather strange."

"If Theo and Frederick were at odds over you, why did they go hunting together?"

Lara had often wondered that herself. "They had managed to avoid each other until the hunt. Theo didn't know Frederick would be there until the last minute, but he'd already accepted the invitation. It would have been bad form for him to decline, so he went. He promised me he wouldn't cause a scene with Frederick. Not many people knew they'd been estranged."

"So no scene, but...murder?"

She nodded. "Yes. When they came to tell me, I knew. I just knew, but the guards and even Frederick all seemed so sincere. He apologized over and over and begged me to forgive him. Told me it was a horrible accident. But then after about three months since Theo's death, Frederick started back sending me gifts and inviting me to attend events with him, and I knew in my heart he'd killed my husband."

"Okay, but what does that have to do with the Benoit?" Gabriel asked.

"Five months after my husband's death, Frederick offered to buy the painting from me. He wanted the Benoit even more than he wanted me, I believe. And now I believe he's willing to kill me to get to that painting."

NINETEEN

"Thank you for meeting me."

The man sitting across the table from Gabriel didn't move or speak. Connor Randall was tall and buff and had a glint in his eyes that didn't match the many disguises Gabriel had seen him in over the past two weeks. He was hardened and stone-faced, but Gabriel had seen his kind over and over in his travels and dealings with not-so-savory people. He'd taken a risk by setting up this meeting, but something had to give. So instead of ignoring the FBI asset, Gabriel had decided they should work together.

"I'm here only because Deidre contacted me in a panic," the man said. "Talk, Murdock."

Gabriel put down his chicory-laced coffee and took one more visual of the Café Du Monde. Malcolm, Deidre and he had talked and made an executive decision to bring Connor Randall up to speed so the man wouldn't go after the princess. Deidre had arranged for him to meet her half brother early this morning.

They were at a table in the back corner, both with a view of the surrounding area. And both were wearing shades and hats. Right now Randall was staring over his Ray-Bans at Gabriel, his slate-colored eyes full of distrust and boredom.

Gabriel charged right in. "Okay, I know why you're in New Orleans, and I think we should quit playing cat and mouse and work together."

"Why am I here?" Randall asked, still not moving.

"The Benoits," Gabriel replied, determined to be as intimidating as Randall seemed to be. "Someone wants all three. Princess Lara Kincade has number one. She might have the others. I don't know. She says she doesn't, and I'm inclined to believe her." Or at least he had been, until a day or so ago. "But they are here somewhere, and we need to find them before she gets herself killed."

"And you'd like a story that's stronger than this coffee."

Gabriel expected Randall had vetted him. He'd done the same so they were even. "I'll give you that, yes. But I came here to do a lightweight exposé and now I'm knee-deep in what could be the art coup of the century."

Randall sat up an inch. "So you're ready to bring the FBI in on this thing?"

"I'm ready for you to quit sulking about and do

your job," Gabriel countered. "I have photos of you at the Kincade Mansion, at the Crescent City Connection on the night of our chicken fight with that other sedan, and I saw you leaving Le Manoir du Jardin in the Quarter. So I know you're just as interested in this as I am. I'm just not sure when you plan to make a move and who you're trying to target, but you need to stay away from Lara Kincade."

Another glinting stare over the dark shades. This was getting ridiculous. "Are you threatening me, Mr. Murdock?"

"No. I'm asking you to help me before the princess does something she'll regret."

Connor Randall lifted his chin. "Such as?"

"Take down Frederick Cordello."

This time, the man sat up straight and took a long sip of his café au lait. "Really now?"

"Really. Now."

"I'll need to get into the gala, of course."

"I'll see to that."

"And you need to stay out of my way, no matter what."

"I can't promise that," Gabriel replied. "I'm committed to this, so I have to protect the princess."

Randall almost snorted. "Admirable, but aren't you a bit out of your league here?"

"Way out of my league," Gabriel admitted. "But I've been here since this all started, and I intend to be here until it ends." He leaned forward, lifting his cup. "I'm pretty sure you know about everything that's occurred so far. If not, I can bring you up to speed."

"I know enough," Randall said. "And again, I'll only agree to help you if you stay out of my way."

"And again," Gabriel retorted, "I can't make that promise."

"Don't worry, Murdock, your princess will be safe. I'm not after her."

Gabriel breathed a sigh of relief. "Good. So you are here for Cordello."

"I didn't say that," Randall replied. "And I can't say any more. Not until the gala at least. That is when the big takedown happens, right?"

"Yes." Gabriel wondered why this high-class FBI asset was here, if not for Cordello. "She thinks Cordello will show up. If he does, she plans to confront him, to get him to confess that he murdered her husband. We don't like it. It's too dangerous."

"Agreed." Randall got up, drained his cup. "Thanks for the coffee. See you at the gala."

"Wait, that's it?" Gabriel asked, keeping his voice low.

"For now," Randall said. "I'll be there and I'll help you. I have a horse in this race, too."

"And what *is* in it for you?" Gabriel asked after grabbing his camera bag.

"I get a stay-out-of-jail card," Randall replied.

"So what's next?"

"I'm going to buy a tux." Connor Randall turned

to leave, then pivoted back around. "Relax, Murdock. I'll catch the bad guy and you'll get the girl."

Gabriel waited until Connor Randall was out of sight before he walked across Decatur Street. Strange meeting. He wasn't sure if he'd helped or hindered things. But at least now he felt as though he'd done something tangible. Taking action made him part of the solution.

And he did want to get the girl, even though his head told him that was a very bad idea. The reasons against falling for Lara were glaring. She was a princess. He was a pauper. She had certain duties and obligations. He ran with the wind. She had everything. He could offer nothing. She got things done. He failed over and over.

But when they were together, none of that seemed to matter. When they were together, the world seemed balanced.

He walked across Jackson Square and once again scanned the entry to the Garden Mansion. Malcolm had told him they'd go over the place again right before the gala, sweeping it for bugs or bombs and checking the surveillance equipment one more time to make sure everything was up to speed. Gabriel had to trust Malcolm on that. He had to trust Lara, too.

Lord, I haven't prayed to You a lot. But I hope You'll grant me this one prayer. Keep her safe. Help me to do the right thing. Help me to see this through. And give me the strength to walk away when it's over.

He took the long way back to the Garden District, walking out his anxieties and concerns, snapping pictures here and there as he went. By the time he'd made it back to Lara's house, Gabriel's head was clear, and he was ready to get on with things.

"Tomorrow night," he said. One way or another, this would end soon.

The next afternoon, Lara stood before the mirror in her bedroom, her reflection staring back at her with a critical eye.

The shimmering cream-colored evening gown sparkled with the glow of a hundred golden threads. Her upswept hair had been sprayed with just a hint of golden glimmer. Her dressy sandals were a shimmering taupe that looked rich but softly elegant.

"Okay, enough with describing myself to myself," she said as she whirled around. "Deidre, you may tell Malcolm I'm ready."

"Yes, ma'am." Deidre wore a severely cut navy gown that draped her body and showed off her curves. Her brown hair was pulled back in a neat ponytail that curled around her neck.

"You look lovely," Deidre said.

"So do you," Lara replied. "I wish we could be excited about this, and I hope we don't regret this night."

Deidre bobbed her head. "You have to do what you need, ma'am, to find some peace of mind."

"Yes, exactly." Lara hadn't been nervous about this night until now. Gabriel would be waiting for her downstairs. Gabriel in a tux and domino mask. She grabbed her evening purse and her own mask, her palms damp, her heartbeat erratic and trembling. She was more afraid of how he made her feel than she was of confronting a killer.

She gave Deidre one last look. "We can't let anyone know that I purposely invited Frederick Cordello here, understood?"

"Yes." Deidre grabbed her clipboard. "I have the RSVP list, and even though his name is not here, I will see to it that he gets through."

"Malcolm knows that if he were to show up, I'm to be contacted immediately, of course."

"Yes, ma'am." Deidre stopped, held her clipboard close. "Be careful, Your Highness."

"I will be." She touched a hand to Deidre's arm. "Thank you for being so loyal."

Deidre nodded and dropped her gaze.

"Is everything all right?" Lara asked, a dread pooling like bayou water in her stomach.

"Yes." Deidre whirled. "We need to go downstairs."

Lara followed Deidre out the bedroom door, her heart booming, her pulse ticking against her temple. For one brief moment, she thought of running down those curving stairs and grabbing Gabriel by the hand and just going far away, forever. But that was a fairy tale kind of dream.

Her reality was that she had an obligation to finish what she'd set out to do in this beautiful, tragic city that she loved. She had to do her duty and she had to confront Frederick Cordello.

Sending up prayers, Lara went from afraid and frantic to stoic and determined. *Dear Father, let me get through this night. Show me what I know to be the truth. Set me free from my guilt and my pain.* She wanted justice, but she also wanted Frederick Cordello to pay for what he'd done. Did she pray to that end? Or did she pray for peace, no matter the outcome of this night?

By the time she reached the last few steps, she had regained her composure. Lifting her head, one hand holding her square, shimmering purse and the other holding the flowing skirt of her dress, she looked down and right into Gabriel's eyes.

Lara's breath hitched in her throat.

The man certainly looked wonderful in a tuxedo.

He stared up at her, his coffee-brown eyes narrowing as his gaze swept over her. He stood straight, the expression on his face one of longing and awe and understanding and pain.

By the time she'd reached the last step, Lara knew she was in love with Gabriel Murdock. Knew it, accepted it and regretted it. After tonight, he wouldn't look at her that way. After tonight, she might never see Gabriel again.

So she decided she would enjoy what little time they had left before she had to face the past and all the things that haunted her still.

Gabriel sat in the back of the big limo with Lara. She'd insisted he ride to the gala with her. He'd packed his camera bag away at his feet, but he intended to use it tonight, if for nothing else, to capture her image in that dress.

He was in love with a princess.

Hadn't seen that one coming.

After all these years of searching the earth for the truth, for reality, for images he could send out to the world, he had finally hit a place where he wanted to stay for a while rather than get in, get the story and get out. He thought about Adina. He'd tried to help her, but even so, he'd had a sense of getting back to the story, a need to get his prints into his editor's hands. That carelessness had cost Adina her life.

Tonight, Gabriel would be focused on one woman. All night long.

The joy of finding someone to love was tempered with the knowledge that he couldn't be honest about his feelings. He wasn't prince material. He didn't want to live in this world of constant espionage and clamoring cameras.

But isn't that the world you've already chosen?

The voice inside his head sounded stern and fatherly.

I'm losing it, he thought. But that voice was right.

He'd been roaming the world in search of chaos, in the path of clamoring cameras. He was one of those clamoring types, always jostling for position to get the story.

"You're so quiet," Lara said, her eyes going dark green in the streetlight shadows that swirled past.

"I'm contemplating," he responded, not sure what to say at this point. "I'm concerned."

She took his hand in hers, the warmth of the solitaire on her left ring finger reminding him that she'd loved and lost.

"Gabriel," she said, her voice whisper soft, "whatever happens tonight, I want you to know how much I've enjoyed getting to know you and being around you. I know your exposé will be wonderful. You're so talented and so considerate. I didn't expect you to be…kind."

He heard the tears in her words. "Is this a brushoff, Princess? Are you telling me goodbye before the fireworks start?"

"No." She looked away, but held his hand still. "No. I mean, we both know—"

"—that it could never work," he finished for her.

She turned back, her eyes misty now. "I don't know. I truly don't. I wouldn't want to tie you down."

"Maybe you could set me free instead."

She glanced over at him, hope shining in her eyes. "I wish we could both be free."

Gabriel couldn't let her go without something to

remember her by. So he leaned in and pulled her into his arms and kissed her, the sweetness of her lips enough for now. But not nearly enough to sustain him when he left her.

They were still in each other's arms when the car stopped.

He let her go, his eyes holding hers. "I'll be by your side all night, Princess. I want to get you in your best light."

She lifted her chin. "I don't think there is enough light to find my good side."

But the look in her eyes told him she wanted him to see all the darkness she held in her heart.

TWENTY

The Benoit was in place. Candles burned in a bright, welcoming glow. Fresh flowers perfumed the night. A long buffet of food tempted the glitzy crowd. A stir of whispers moved through the big ballroom on the second floor of Le Manoir du Jardin. All eyes moved from the painting centered over the fireplace to the woman who stood at the door.

"The princess is here."

Gabriel heard the excited ripple. Lara glanced over at him, and for an instant he saw a spark of doubt and fear in the slits of her glittering, feathered mask. If at this moment he took her and escaped out the open French doors and hurried down those stairs, would she run away with him?

But he couldn't do that. She wouldn't do that. Instead, he stood back and allowed her to bask in the glow of bringing so many important people together in one place. This fundraiser had been well planned and well published. Everyone, from the governor to the members of both the state senate and house, was here. A few celebrities mingled with the upper crust of New Orleans society, all wearing festive masks that partially covered their faces. The room was packed with sparkling, glittering people who only had one thought on their minds. They all wanted to meet the princess.

Gabriel stood back and snapped discreet pictures as she moved into position to endure the receiving line. She had seemed reluctant in the car, but now she shined like a star with that serene smile, her head inclined, her pearls and diamonds flashing. He couldn't see her eyes, but he suspected they were watching and waiting.

This was what a princess did.

But Lara, his princess, also laughed and made tea and toast and planned out her days and occasionally wore jeans and a white T-shirt. The Lara he knew was a woman, through and through. A woman he could laugh with and love for a long, long time.

Dear God, how can I protect her when she's putting herself in harm's way? How can I show her that I can love her and that I want to make her forget the horrors of the past?

Could he forget his own horrors? he wondered. Gabriel watched and waited, his heart pumping adrenaline and his mind swamped with all the scenarios he'd imagined inside his head. Deidre stood nearby wearing a simple black mask.

"Mr. Armond is here," she whispered to Gabriel. Gabriel followed the man toward Lara, his camera the perfect cover. He took her picture with Louis Armond, but the older man seemed enthralled and glad to see her again. He'd come alone, which was odd. Gabriel kept that tidbit inside his mind.

A few more dignitaries followed, and Gabriel took shots of each one. Then he heard Deidre inhale.

"Your half brother has arrived," he said to her on a low whisper.

"I can see that." Deidre stared at the open arch leading to the hallway. "He always did look nice cleaned up."

Connor Randall strolled through the doors as if he owned the place. With a sly wink through his skinny mask at his half sister and a slight frown at Gabriel, he moved through the receiving line and waited his turn to shake hands with the princess. When he reached Lara, he made a polite move, smiled at her and kept moving.

"Has she ever met your brother?" Gabriel asked Deidre.

"Never. The two had no reason to cross paths."

Gabriel was ready for this mystery to end so, as Connor had suggested, he could get the girl. Now if they both could figure out the bad guy.

Gabriel watched as Connor approached Louis Armond. The Frenchman smiled and chatted with Connor, but there was a sense of urgency to their conversation. Gabriel snapped a picture, capturing the two men in an intimate conversation.

What was up with that? Did they know each other?

Then Gabriel glanced at Lara and saw her staring at the door, her expression frozen with anticipation. He turned, but Deidre grabbed his coat sleeve.

"That's Frederick Cordello," Deidre said on a slow breath. "I can't believe he actually came, even though the princess personally invited him. I have to go and clear him."

Gabriel turned back toward Lara. Maybe she regretted that invitation. Her face told a tale of terror. Her eyes slanted through the opening ovals of the mask as a piercing frown fell like a curtain across her features. But before Frederick had made it through the door, the frown was gone and her eyes once again were a serene blue-green.

Gabriel breathed deep and got himself together. He moved closer to Lara. He saw Malcolm doing the same across the way.

As Cordello approached Lara, the whole room seemed to go quiet with anticipation. Did this crowd recognize that this was the man who'd "accidentally" shot Lara's husband?

By the time Cordello was reaching out a hand to Lara, Gabriel was right in front of them. He snapped several pictures of them together. Lara remained calm and polite, her demure smile frozen in place. When Frederick reached out as if to hug her, Lara stepped back and took the man's hands in her own, a clear sign that she wasn't yet ready to embrace her enemy.

But a buzz of whispers moved through the room like a swarm of locusts out for tender stalks. All of those reporters waiting outside would no doubt find someone to tell them what had happened here tonight. People would trade their souls to be inside this room. Gabriel only wanted to take Lara and get away from this overdressed, hyped-up crowd. To get her away from this need for revenge.

Frederick Cordello said something in Lara's ear, then moved on. Lara nodded and smiled.

Had Lara decided to call off her vendetta?

Gabriel watched her while she watched Frederick Cordello. Her gaze stayed on the tall, red-haired man dressed in a tailored tuxedo. And she kept glancing back to him between the handshaking and the last people waiting in the receiving line. When she realized the room was full and she could move about, she started across the room.

Gabriel finally made it to her side. "Are you all right?"

"I'm fine," she said, but it came out as a breathless whisper.

The music started. The orchestra began, and the soothing sounds of Bach seemed to bring down the tension that had permeated the room.

Without thinking, he handed his camera to Deidre and pulled Lara into his arms. "Let's dance."

"You didn't ask," Lara said as he swept her around in a waltz.

"You didn't say no," Gabriel replied, his eyes holding hers. "Is it over now, Lara?"

"What?"

"Your need for justice?"

"The night is young, Gabriel," she replied. "But for now I intend to enjoy dancing with you."

Gabriel didn't question her any further. She was right. The night had only just begun. And he wouldn't be able to rest until everyone was gone and he was alone with this woman.

In the meantime, he intended to keep her alive.

Lara glanced around the crowded room. For two hours, she'd endured anticipation and regret. The silent auction was in full swing, with everyone trying to outbid each other. The live auction would begin in a few minutes. After that, she'd make her move to confront Frederick Cordello. Then it would all be over, at last.

"Would you like something to eat?" Gabriel asked as she swept by him.

She shook her head. "I had a bite here and there. I'm still not quite over that spell I had a few days ago."

"Are you afraid of the food, Lara?"

"No." She laughed away his concerns. "I'm just

not very hungry." Switching gears, she asked, "Are you having a good time?"

He frowned against his black mask. "Oh, yes. As much as one can have a good time while worrying about keeping a princess safe and watching out for an expensive piece of art and wondering which one of these men is after you and/or the art."

"Dramatic. No wonder your pictures entertain and inform the masses."

"I'm not being dramatic. I'm being serious."

Lara's heart bumped against the boning in her gown. "I know that, but I enjoyed dancing with you."

"That's all you can say? You enjoyed dancing with me? Why don't you tell me what's really going on inside your beautiful mind?"

She swallowed, prayed. "I'm fine, Gabriel." Then she put a hand to his face. "You don't have to worry about me."

"Easy for you to say."

Dropping her hand, she looked at her watch. "I have to go. It's time for the live auction."

"I'm right behind you."

Lara made her way to the front of the room. Deidre took her cue and hit the podium with a gavel. The auctioneer followed suit and waited for Lara to speak.

"Thank you all for coming," she said, her poised shell hiding the tremors inside her heart. "This event will help us to continue building Kincade houses all over New Orleans. I can assure you that every penny we make here goes straight to helping people find new homes. Thank you for your support, and I wish you the best."

She went to her seat and waited while the colorful auctioneer started the bidding. It didn't take long for all the prime pieces to go, but she was thrilled the bidding went so high. When it was over, she stood to encourage everyone to continue enjoying the party.

Deidre beat her to the mike. "We'd like to present Her Royal Highness with a special surprise tonight."

Lara saw Gabriel move toward her. She didn't like surprises. He stood right by her.

Two chefs dressed like jesters rolled in a giant cake shaped like a house. The lettering read *Thank you, Princess Lara.*

Lara breathed a sigh of relief. She looked at Gabriel and he actually smiled. "You should have the first slice."

Apparently, the two masked chefs agreed. One of the men cut Lara a huge piece off the corner and bowed his head, indicating he wanted her to have the cake.

Lara took it and broke into it with the fork. She really wasn't hungry, but it would be rude to refuse this generous gift. Just one bite.

She reached the fork to her lips when the other chef whipped off his hat and mask and ran toward her, then knocked the plate of cake to the floor. "Don't eat that, Princess. It's poisoned."

"Herbert?" Lara heard herself as if from a long distance. "Herbert, is it you?"

Before the chef could answer, a shot echoed over the walls, and Herbert fell to the floor. Then pandemonium took over as everyone started pushing toward the exits.

Lara felt herself being pushed and pulled. Gabriel had her in his arms, trying to get her out the French doors to the upper balcony. "Hold on to me. Don't let go."

They pushed through the doors, and he tugged her to one corner. "Are you all right?"

"Yes. But Herbert—"

"I don't care about that right now." Gabriel searched the screaming crowd. "Where is Malcolm?"

"I didn't see him." Lara moved to go back inside, but Gabriel held her back. "No. Let's get you down to the car."

He pulled her down the stairs toward the garden.

At the bottom, a man blocked their way, then lifted a gun toward them. "Not so fast, Lara, dear. We have some unfinished business."

Lara held to Gabriel, hatred filling her heart. "Frederick." She tugged away from Gabriel. "What do you want?"

"The Benoit, of course," Frederick Cordello said.

"Your stupid Herbert has messed up my original plan, but no matter. Now if you'll both come with me."

Gabriel didn't have his camera. He only had his cell phone, and they'd probably take that from him once they discovered it. But he had to try to alert Malcolm and the police. Somehow.

"Where are you taking us?" he asked as Cordello took them down a winding corridor that must lead to the basement of the big house.

"The wine cellar," Cordello replied. "No one is supposed to be down here, and I don't have time to look for a better hiding place. It's amazing what money can buy. Even a scared, overweight chef with gambling debts. Also amazing that he risked his life for you."

"You've managed to escape a lot of situations," Lara retorted. "I wish I had my purse." She glanced at Gabriel.

Gabriel thought that was an odd statement until he remembered something she'd said in passing the other night.

I have a gun.

Did she have a gun in her purse? Or did she have one on her now? The woman never ceased to amaze him. He put his hand in his pocket, pulled out his phone.

"Just like a woman, worried about her purse,"

Frederick retorted. "That won't matter if you don't get me that Benoit. Wait, I mean all three of the Benoits. I saw them. Theo flaunted them, but refused to let me buy one. Now I'll take them."

Lara seemed as calm as ever. "How can I do that when you have me down here?"

Cordello paced back and forth, glancing up the stairs, where voices and footsteps echoed.

Gabriel gazed around the dank, dark basement. It smelled musty with decay. The remnants of old wine bottles lining a rustic shelf shined in the dull gray light from a small, dusty window. A few barrels and some storage boxes. A tiny window with bars over it. No way to escape. He shifted his gaze to his hidden phone and scrolled, slowly, carefully, until he found Malcolm's number. All he could do was press the call button and pray.

Cordello ignored Gabriel and handed Lara a phone of her own. "Call this number. Tell them to bring the Benoit."

Lara glared at him, but Gabriel pressed her hand. "Do it, Lara."

Frederick smirked at them. "Yes, Lara, do as you're told. You always have."

Lara pressed the call button, her gaze piercing Cordello. "Hello. Yes. Bring the Benoit to the basement. Now. Follow the winding stairs to the wine cellar."

"Who answered?" Gabriel asked, trying to buy time until he could get them out of this situation.

"I don't know." Lara glanced from him to Frederick. "So you kept calling, leaving things to scare me. Did you leave all those things to convince me? Did you try to kill me?"

"Of course I tried to kill you. Or at least tried to scare you to death." He circled them, his eyes glowing in the muted light. "I want what Theo promised me years ago, and I had to get you out of the way. But you never could take a hint."

"The Benoit?" Lara asked, edging closer to Gabriel. "It's always about that painting."

"Those paintings," Cordello shouted. "I need all three."

Gabriel felt it before he realized it. She pressed her foot against his. Her ankle. Gabriel pressed back and felt something bulky there above her shimmering high-heeled sandals.

She did have a gun! Strapped to her leg.

His princess had come here tonight with a whole different agenda, after all. Now what?

"Why do you want it so much?" Lara asked, her body slowly slumping. She staggered, stood against Gabriel. "I'm sorry. I'm so dizzy."

Gabriel went into action, pulling her into his arms. "You poisoned the cake? Did you plan on poisoning everyone?"

Frederick laughed out loud. "I didn't do anything to the cake, but I let your dear chef Herbert think he'd baked poison into the cake. Great chef, but no personality. I needed a distraction, and I knew he'd cave, but he got ahead of himself, and now it's plan B. He was driving me nuts anyway. He didn't want his precious princess to die."

"What if he'd let her eat the cake?" Gabriel asked, holding Lara, trying to protect her, praying she didn't go for that pistol.

Frederick walked to the stairs and glanced up. "I guess I would have had to shoot someone else." He shrugged, walked back. "They should be down soon."

Lara held to Gabriel. "Not if my team finds them."

"Your team?" He hissed a laugh, his gun pointing toward them. "Your incompetent, stupid team. A bunch of bumbling idiots. I got past your team several times. Oh, wait. I bribed some of your team. If you want them to be trustworthy, you might want to give them a raise."

When they heard footsteps and voices, Frederick ran to the foot of the stairs. "Hurry."

Lara lifted her skirt and quickly pulled out the little gun. Gabriel glanced at Cordello and back to her. "Don't."

But Lara wasn't listening. She waited, pressed against him, her right hand down by her side.

Finally, two men came down the stairs, carrying the Benoit.

"Set it right there," Frederick said, his voice full of glee.

They placed it against an old chair. The light

from the street gleamed over it like a halo. Gabriel stared at the painting, wondering why Cordello had sent the other two renditions. And then he saw it. Right there as plain as day.

And he finally knew where the other two Benoits had been all along.

TWENTY-ONE

Lara held the dainty pistol like a lifeline. She'd use it.

She'd planned to use it. For as long as she could remember, she'd waited for this moment. She'd gone so far as to take it out of her purse and strap it to her leg. How sick was that?

Not sick. She'd known since the first phone call with Cordello that this moment would come. Her only regret was that Frederick had tricked her and beat her to the punch. He'd whispered in her ear, "We need to talk after this is over."

Now, *now,* she would talk. She'd show him he couldn't hurt the people she loved. But inside her heart, she trembled and wondered, what had become of her?

Dear Lord, have I lost my soul? My ability to love? Had she used Gabriel as a means to an end? Had she forced her staff to be a part of this—killing another human being?

She couldn't take her eyes off the man she'd

loathed for so long. But she didn't want to see the person she'd become because of her anger and grief.

He stood staring at her, the gun in his hand raised. "Where are the other two, Lara?"

"I don't know," she replied. "I don't know. And I don't care. Take that one. It's only brought me pain."

Cordello advanced. "I want all three, and I think you know where they are."

"I don't have them," Lara shouted. "I've never had them."

"She's telling the truth," Gabriel said. "Why don't you take the Benoit and go?"

"It's not that easy," Frederick replied, his whole body jittery and jumpy. "I have obligations—"

"He certainly does."

They all turned to find Louis Armond standing on the stairs. "He has an obligation to me, Your Highness."

"Not you, too?" Lara glanced at Gabriel, then turned back to Armond. "Did all of my husband's friends betray him?"

"I haven't betrayed anyone," Armond said as he came down the stairs, two burly men with their own big guns behind him. "I've been searching for the two lost Benoits for a very long time. You see, I'm a direct descendant of the man who painted these portraits, and I can prove it through provenance. I have the official record of the chronology of owner-ship. And I know how much the trio is worth. Your friend Mr. Cordello has promised to deliver them in return for me forgiving his rather excessive loans."

Gabriel shifted in front of Lara. "Jacques Benoit is your ancestor? So you want the paintings, but you haven't been terrorizing the princess?"

Armond shook his head. "No. Theo Kincade and I were good friends. He was a kind man and always willing to listen. He didn't judge. But that was one of his biggest flaws. He trusted too much."

"So do I," Lara replied. "I trusted Frederick and he killed my husband." She was about to raise her own gun when they heard more footsteps.

"How many people did you invite to this party, Armond?" Frederick asked. "I told you I'd find the missing Benoits, and I think I have. No need to bring in anyone else."

"Your time is up," Louis Armond replied. "Your debts have to be paid, one way or another."

"He's right about that," another voice called. "And I'm here to collect."

A tall, dark-haired man came down the stairs. "Let me introduce myself. I'm Connor Randall. And my friends from the FBI—who have snipers trained on both of you right now—tell me that neither of you can lay claim to the Benoit. I've come to collect it for them. It's considered to be stolen art."

"Then it belongs to me," Armond said, motioning to his two men to take the painting. "You promised me you'd help me, Randall."

"And I did," Connor Randall replied. "We all helped each other. Nice, isn't it?"

"I won't let you have the Benoit," Frederick screamed. Then he started shooting.

After that, everyone started moving at once. Gabriel grabbed Lara and dragged her toward the door. "Randall, you could have given me some warning."

"I tried," the other man replied, his gun in the air.

They made it past the fighting men surrounding the painting, and Gabriel had her on the stairs. Lara stopped. "You know him?"

Gabriel looked guilty. "That's Deidre's half brother."

Shocked, Lara realized she'd been duped again and this time by Gabriel. "What? Why?"

Before she could find out the truth, a shot rang out and Gabriel whirled in front of her.

And took a bullet meant for her. He grabbed his arm where blood bubbled out over his fingers. "Go, Lara. Get out of here."

"No!" Lara screamed, glanced around as someone pulled Gabriel away. "No!" Arms held her, but she wanted to find Gabriel.

Lara still clutched her own gun, and without thinking, she lifted her right hand and looked straight into Frederick Cordello's eyes.

But she couldn't do it. She couldn't kill another human being.

"This is for my husband," she said before pulling the trigger. "And this is for Gabriel."

She shot in the air again and again until there were no bullets left. But when Frederick kept coming, unwounded, and hurled himself toward her, another shot rang out. Cordello fell to the floor, his unseeing eyes staring at the Benoit.

Connor Randall had killed Frederick Cordello.

The next thing she knew, Malcolm had her upstairs and in a chair. "I'm fine," she said over and over, tears streaming down her face, her hand in Deidre's. "Gabriel. Find Gabriel."

Lara sat and prayed while police and paramedics and curious people moved all around her. She'd caused this. She'd brought this on all of them. And Gabriel had paid a high price for helping her.

She'd never told him how much she loved him. And now it was too late.

Three weeks later, Gabriel once again entered the tightly patrolled gates to Lara's home in the Garden District. He'd had no word from her in all that time, but Malcolm and Deidre had kept him informed, right along with several papers, both local and national. The princess was in seclusion after her harrowing experience before and during the gala. The Benoit was safely back in her home until the authorities could decide to whom it belonged. Frederick Cordello was dead, shot by Connor Randall just before he tried to kill Princess Lara. Connor

Randall refused to talk to the press, but the FBI had confirmed that Frederick Cordello had harassed and terrorized the princess, had kidnapped her chef and had killed the chef's roommate. They'd also confirmed that they'd asked the local police to stand by and not blow their secretive investigation. Louis Armond had been cleared of any wrongdoing since he'd been cooperating with the FBI, but he'd held a press conference stating that Theodore Kincade had promised him he knew where the two missing Benoits were located, though he'd been killed before he could reveal that information. So Louis Armond had gone after Frederick Cordello and found his weakness—money to pay for his extravagant lifestyle.

Armond demanded a new investigation and answers—and a possible long, drawn-out court battle.

Meantime, Gabriel had finished his photo exposé, added commentary and now held a freshly printed copy of *Real World News* in his hand, to give to the princess.

If she'd see him. If they'd let her see him.

He was allowed inside the gate with a phone call from Deidre. "She'll see you now, sir."

Gabriel waited at the front door, then walked inside when Deidre opened it. "Hi," he said to the still-shy girl.

"Hello. We've missed you. So glad your wound is all better."

He glanced at the big bandage on his left arm. "Me, too. How's your brother?"

"Gone again. Off to finish up his time with the FBI."

"How's the princess?"

When he heard high heels clicking against the hardwood floors, he turned, swallowed and stared at the woman he'd fallen in love with.

Princess Lara Barrington Kincade. Pumps and pearls and a hesitant smile.

"The princess is still very angry with everyone around her," Lara replied, polite and aloof and gorgeous. "Especially with one Gabriel Murdock. They told me you had left after you were released from the hospital. Just like that—gone."

"I can explain."

"I can't wait to hear your version of why everyone kept Connor Randall's true identity from me."

"It's the same as the rest. He couldn't blow his cover." Gabriel waited a beat. "All things considered, just about everybody involved in this mess had secrets, including you, Princess. I hope you can forgive all of us. Especially one Gabriel Murdock."

She put her hand under her chin. "Hmm." Then she dropped her hand down and ran the rest of the way and fell into his arms. "I can't remember why I was mad to begin with."

Gabriel kissed her, held her, breathed in the essence of her. "Hello, Princess."

"Hello, Gabriel."

* * *

Later, after they'd had lunch prepared by a jolly and very much alive Herbert, and she'd made sure Gabriel was truly okay and in good shape, and they'd glanced over the pictures of her life, Lara turned to Gabriel and smiled. "You did a good job."

"It's the real story, good and bad." He got up to stand in front of the Benoit. "There is one thing I left out, however."

"What now?" she asked, rising to pace toward him, happy to be breathing the same air with him.

He pointed to the beautiful painting. "You've had all three all along."

"What?" Lara stared at the Benoit. How many times had she done that, stared at the painting but seen nothing but her own bitterness and regret? "Explain, please?"

Gabriel pointed to the clouds in the painting. "I saw it in the moonlight there in the old wine cellar. It's hard to see in the wrong light, but in the two clouds just above the lone shepherd—" he pulled her in front of him, leaned his head over her shoulder "—there is this silvery kind of etching of the other clouds in the two other paintings. I think that wasn't on the original, and I think that's a clue. Do you see it?"

"Just barely," Lara said, moving so the light shined differently on the painting. "But that doesn't mean—"

"The other two are behind this one, Lara."

"No." She turned to stare up at him. "How do you know?"

"I did some more research, and it just makes sense. It's a trinity. Someone, maybe Theo, had the good sense to have the other two mounted behind the first one. Safe and together."

"Can we take it apart?"

"You'd need an art expert, but I'm thinking Louis Armond would be willing to provide one."

"You are amazing," she said with a smile.

"I've got a surprise for you," he replied. "If you feel like venturing out into the garden."

"I'd love walking outside with you, but I don't like surprises."

"You'll like this one."

So they went out the sunroom door, and Gabriel took her to an old stone fountain. "Is this your idea of a romantic setting?" she asked, laughing.

He pointed to a big cardboard box sitting on the path.

"No, this is my idea of helping you to relax. Open the box."

Wondering what he was talking about, Lara did as he'd asked. "I see old dishes. Lots of old dishes."

"Remember when you said you often dreamed of throwing plates?"

She started laughing again, her face crinkling, her eyes watering, her stomach tightening. She hadn't really laughed in so long. So very long.

"Oh, Gabriel, I love you so much."

He tugged her into his arms. "I tried to stay away, tried to forget you. But…I love you. You're hard to forget."

She pulled back to stare into his eyes. "Can we make this work?"

"I'm willing to try. I don't have much to offer. I'm no prince."

"You're my prince," she said, a finger to his lips. "We've survived a lot in the past few weeks. I think we can handle everything else. With God's help, of course."

"Amen. Wanna throw some plates?"

"Yes." Lara picked a pretty floral-patterned one and tossed it at the old fountain. It shattered with a pleasant sound that did ease the stress of the past couple of months.

Then she turned to Gabriel. "I was so afraid I'd lost you."

He threw a plain white plate, watching as it crashed and fell away from the hard stone. "Never."

Lara wrapped her arms around his neck and kissed him again. "I hope you won't be bored with me."

"Never," he repeated. "You are a constant adventure, Princess. I can't wait to get started."

Together they threw plates and laughed and planned and…enjoyed being free. Lara decided this was a picture she could cherish the rest of her life.

* * * * *

Dear Reader,

Isn't it amazing how we treasure things here on earth? We collect clutter and hold it close, afraid to let it go. I've learned all about this since I moved from a large private home to a small town house. I had stored up a lot of treasures, but getting rid of some of the clutter in my house helped me to get some of the clutter out of my life and my head, too.

Princess Lara Kincade held the treasure of God's love and the love and devotion she felt toward her deceased husband. She didn't care so much about being a princess. She only wanted that kind of love back in her life. When Gabriel Murdock walked into her life, her loyalties began to shift, causing her guilt and grief. But Gabriel saw the real treasure and pursued Lara while trying to keep her alive. They both had to give up a lot to find each other.

I hope you enjoyed this story. And I hope that if you're suffering from too much clutter in your life, you'll consider the treasure of God's love and grace. It's a beautiful story, painted with a broad stroke. Don't miss the details that Christ has painted for us.

Until next time, may the angels watch over you. Always.

Lenora Worth

Questions for Discussion

1. Have you ever dreamed of being a princess? Do you think it's all glamour and excitement?

2. Even though Lara had a charming life, she was still lonely and miserable. Do you think she had a right to feel sorry for herself in spite of all the amenities she was offered?

3. How did Lara help calm Gabriel's nomadic frame of mind? Do you think a man like Gabriel can settle down?

4. What made Gabriel more than just a photographer? Do you think he overstepped his position, or that he was just doing the right thing in trying to protect Lara?

5. I use New Orleans as a setting in a lot of my stories. Do you believe this beautiful city needs redemption or can you see the good in a place such as this?

6. The art world is full of murky characters and greedy people. Have you ever owned something that was worth a lot of money? Did you show this item off or try to find out its value?

Do you think this kind of treasure matters in God's eyes?

7. How did Lara's faith keep her grounded? How did that help Gabriel to see the truth of God's love?

8. Lara had a devoted staff, but Gabriel didn't trust anyone. They had two very different attitudes. Are you more like Lara or maybe more skeptical like Gabriel?

9. What did you think about Deidre's intriguing brother, Connor Randall? He was doing penance for his crimes. Do you think he can be reformed?

10. Why did everyone want the Benoit painting so much? What is it about hidden treasures that makes reasonable men become dangerous?

11. What did you see in the painting as described on these pages? Was the plight of the Arcadians depicted in a way that showed their suffering? Did you like the dream-within-a-dream form of art? How did the portrait show God's love?

12. Do you think art has a place in faith? How has art helped you in your own faith?

13. Was Lara fair to Gabriel? Did she push him away too much? Did she deliberately court danger just to prove herself? Have you ever pushed away someone who was trying to help you?

14. Lara shared a secret desire with Gabriel early in the story. At the end, Gabriel gave her that one wish. Did you like that scene? Have you ever wanted to throw something out of frustration?

15. How did the rule of three play into this story? Did you understand the reference to the Father, Son and Holy Ghost?

REQUEST YOUR FREE BOOKS!

2 FREE RIVETING INSPIRATIONAL NOVELS
PLUS 2 FREE MYSTERY GIFTS

Love Inspired
SUSPENSE

YES! Please send me 2 FREE Love Inspired® Suspense novels and my 2 FREE mystery gifts (gifts are worth about $10). After receiving them, if I don't wish to receive any more books, I can return the shipping statement marked "cancel." If I don't cancel, I will receive 4 brand-new novels every month and be billed just $4.74 per book in the U.S. or $5.24 per book in Canada. That's a savings of at least 21% off the cover price. It's quite a bargain! Shipping and handling is just 50¢ per book in the U.S. and 75¢ per book in Canada.* I understand that accepting the 2 free books and gifts places me under no obligation to buy anything. I can always return a shipment and cancel at any time. Even if I never buy another book, the two free books and gifts are mine to keep forever.

123/323 IDN F5AN

Name	(PLEASE PRINT)	
Address		Apt. #
City	State/Prov.	Zip/Postal Code

Signature (if under 18, a parent or guardian must sign)

Mail to the **Harlequin®** Reader Service:
IN U.S.A.: P.O. Box 1867, Buffalo, NY 14240-1867
IN CANADA: P.O. Box 609, Fort Erie, Ontario L2A 5X3

**Are you a current subscriber to Love Inspired Suspense books
and want to receive the larger-print edition?
Call 1-800-873-8635 or visit www.ReaderService.com.**

* Terms and prices subject to change without notice. Prices do not include applicable taxes. Sales tax applicable in N.Y. Canadian residents will be charged applicable taxes. Offer not valid in Quebec. This offer is limited to one order per household. Not valid for current subscribers to Love Inspired Suspense books. All orders subject to credit approval. Credit or debit balances in a customer's account(s) may be offset by any other outstanding balance owed by or to the customer. Please allow 4 to 6 weeks for delivery. Offer available while quantities last.

Your Privacy—The Harlequin® Reader Service is committed to protecting your privacy. Our Privacy Policy is available online at www.ReaderService.com or upon request from the Harlequin Reader Service.
We make a portion of our mailing list available to reputable third parties that offer products we believe may interest you. If you prefer that we not exchange your name with third parties, or if you wish to clarify or modify your communication preferences, please visit us at www.ReaderService.com/consumerchoice or write to us at Harlequin Reader Service Preference Service, P.O. Box 9062, Buffalo, NY 14269. Include your complete name and address.

LISDIR13R